THE BIG STING

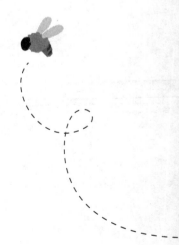

Books by

RACHELLE DELANEY

Alice Fleck's Recipes for Disaster

Clara Voyant

The Bonaventure Adventures

The Metro Dogs of Moscow
The Circus Dogs of Prague

The Ship of Lost Souls
The Guardians of Island X
The Hunt for the Panther

THE BIG STING

RACHELLE DELANEY

tundra

Paperback edition published by Tundra Books, 2024
First published in hardcover, 2023

Tundra Books, an imprint of Tundra Book Group,
a division of Penguin Random House of Canada Limited

*Publisher's note: This book is a work of fiction. Names, characters, places and incidents
either are the product of the author's imagination or are used fictitiously, and any
resemblance to actual persons living or dead, events, or locales is entirely coincidental.*

Library and Archives Canada Cataloguing in Publication

Title: The big sting / Rachelle Delaney.
Names: Delaney, Rachelle, author.
Description: Previously published in 2023.
Identifiers: Canadiana 20230198538 | ISBN 9780735269323 (softcover)
Classification: LCC PS8607.E48254 B54 2024 | DDC jC813/.6—dc23

Published simultaneously in the United States of America by Tundra Books
of Northern New York, an imprint of Tundra Book Group, a division of
Penguin Random House of Canada Limited
Library of Congress Control Number: 2022933335

Edited by Lynne Missen
Cover designed by Emma Dolan
The text was set in Baskerville Pro Regular.

Printed in Canada

www.penguinrandomhouse.ca

3 4 5   28 27 26 25 24

Penguin
Random House
tundra | TUNDRA BOOKS

CHAPTER 1

Leo woke to the sound of a grumble. Or maybe a huff. A grumble-huff? Blinking in the early morning light, he wondered if there were such a thing as a grumble-huff.

He lay very still, holding his breath, until he heard the noise again. It wasn't Lizzie snoring, though that wouldn't have been unusual. His sister was sleeping quietly for once, in the twin-sized bed across the room from his.

Could it be an animal? he wondered. Could there be grumble-huffing animals in the walls of Grandpa's house? According to Mom, the house was almost a hundred years old, so it was entirely possible. He shivered.

Then he heard the noise again, this time followed by the sound of someone stomping down the hallway. Which could only mean one thing: the grumble-huffing animal was Grandpa himself. Because Grandpa didn't walk. He *stomped*.

Leo pulled the covers up to his chin and resolved to stay in bed until he heard Mom or Dad emerge from their room at the end of the hallway.

Except . . .

Except now he had to pee.

No, you don't, he told himself, and he tried to think of something else—something calming, something that had nothing to do with the bathroom. Like playing the *Applewood Acres* games with his best friend, Santos. Over the past year they'd spent dozens if not hundreds of hours at Santos's computer planting and harvesting a virtual farm in *Applewood Acres,* protecting it from marauding wild pigs in *Applewood Acres 2: Hog Wild* and tending to their own apiary (a fancy word for beehives) in *Applewood Acres 3: What's the Buzz?* They'd been eagerly awaiting the release of *Applewood Acres 4: Shenanigoats* for months, so *of course* it had come out the very day Leo had to fly across the country to spend a week on a tiny island with a grumble-huffing grandpa who didn't even have an internet connection in his hundred-year-old house.

"Who doesn't have the internet?" Leo sighed up at the ceiling.

He still had to pee.

They'd arrived late the night before, so his mental map of Grandpa's house was still sketchy. But he was fairly certain the bathroom was one door down from the room he and Lizzie were sharing. Across from the bathroom was

Grandpa's bedroom, and beside that was the room where Mom and Dad were sleeping. It wasn't far—he could probably dash to the bathroom, do his business and dash back to bed in four minutes, maybe less. But it was not without risk. Specifically, the risk of running into Grandpa.

"Is he always this grumpy?" Leo had asked Mom and Dad the night before when they came to tuck him in. Lizzie was already fast asleep.

"No," Mom had said at the same time Dad said, "Oh yeah." Mom frowned at Dad and he shrugged.

"Don't take it personally, Leo." Dad dropped a kiss on his forehead. "It's just his way."

"He's grieving," Mom added as she switched off the light. "And grief is . . . well, complicated. But he's happy we're here. He just has a hard time showing it."

Leo had a hard time believing that. But even if it were true, he didn't want to face Grandpa, with his glaring green eyes and perpetual frown, alone.

And yet. He really had to pee.

When he couldn't hold it any longer, he slipped out of bed and tiptoed across the room—not that there was any chance of waking Lizzie, who'd never met a noise she couldn't sleep through. She'd even slept through the hour-long ferry ride from Vancouver to Heron Island despite the thunderous engine and the waves that rocked the boat from side to side. Mom and Dad hadn't wanted to wake her, so they'd all stayed in the rental car, and Leo had tried not to think about the deep, dark water churning beneath them. He and Santos had once spent several weeks exploring the ocean in a game called *Neptune 3: The Deepest Dive*, so he knew a thing or two about how incredibly dark and unbearably cold it was down there.

He opened the bedroom door and made sure the coast was clear before creeping down the hall toward the bathroom. His toes curled on the cool wood, and he missed the soft carpet in their condo at home. He hurried to the bathroom and pushed open the door, only to discover that his mental map wasn't just sketchy, but completely wrong.

For there was Grandpa, standing in his bedroom, clutching a giant book to his chest.

Leo yelped and stumbled back.

Grandpa's green eyes widened, then narrowed. "Bathroom?" he said.

Leo gulped and nodded.

Grandpa pointed at the door across the hall. Leo spun around, dove into the actual bathroom and shut the door.

After he'd peed and washed his hands, he stood quietly at the door, listening for grumble-huffs in the hallway. Hearing none, he opened the door, only to find Grandpa still standing in his bedroom doorway, staring at him.

Leo yelped again and Grandpa shushed him. Then he motioned for Leo to follow him and stomped off down the hall.

"Oh no," Leo whispered. What could he possibly want? Wishing he'd never gotten out of bed, he followed Grandpa down the hall into the kitchen.

The walls in Grandpa's kitchen were painted school bus yellow, and with the morning sun streaming through the window over the sink, the room practically glowed. It was the sunniest room Leo had ever seen, which was funny because Grandpa was the stormiest person he'd ever met.

Grandpa picked a mug up off the kitchen table, sipped from it, then set it back down with a thud. "How are you with bees?" he asked.

Leo blinked. "Bees?"

"Bees," Grandpa repeated.

Leo opened his mouth, then shut it. He'd never considered how he was with bees. In *Applewood Acres 3: What's the Buzz?* he and Santos had managed fifty beehives. Or they'd *tried* to, until an unseasonable cold snap killed nearly all their bees, costing them thousands of points.

But those were virtual bees. Real-life bees could sting. Leo had never been stung before, so he wasn't sure if he was allergic like Santos, whose face would inflate like a balloon when he got stung. Leo had never actually seen this happen, but it sounded awful. So that was a mark against bees.

Of course, bees weren't all bad—in fact, they were very important. Earlier that year, in fifth grade science class, Leo's teacher had asked the students to list everything they'd eaten the previous day, then cross off all foods that required bees for pollination—everything from apples to peanut butter to the chocolate chips in a granola bar. Without bees, Leo had concluded, he'd be living off mostly cheese. But then his teacher reminded him that cows and goats ate grasses that needed bees for pollination, which meant—

"Leo." Grandpa snapped his fingers.

"Hmm?" Leo blinked, returning to the sunny kitchen and Grandpa's cold stare.

Grandpa sighed. "I was going to ask you to come with me on an important mission. I thought you might be the right person."

"You did?" Leo was surprised. "What is it?"

Grandpa set his giant book down on the table, where Leo could read the title: *Everything Bees.* "I have to tell them something."

"Tell who?"

Grandpa pointed to the book. "The bees."

"Tell the *bees*?" Leo looked from Grandpa to the book, then back to Grandpa. "Tell them what? And how?" In all his time as a virtual beekeeper, Leo had never once spoken to his bees.

Grandpa frowned. "You ask a lot of questions."

Leo nodded. Everyone said that.

"On second thought, maybe I should go alone." Grandpa took a crumpled brown hat off a rack near the back door and set it on his head.

"No, wait." Leo made a quick mental list of the risks involved in this mysterious mission. The greatest risk, as far as he knew, was getting stung. Would Grandpa know what to do if Leo turned out to be allergic and his face inflated like a balloon?

"You don't have to come. It was just an idea." Grandpa picked *Everything Bees* up off the table and headed for the door, which opened onto a porch overlooking the field behind the house.

Leo bit his lip. On the other hand, he *did* want to see Grandpa's farm—he'd promised Santos he'd let him know if it looked anything like Applewood Acres.

And more importantly, Grandpa had said he'd thought Leo was the right person to come with him on *an important mission*. Had anyone ever thought that before? Leo highly doubted it.

He imagined Lizzie's face when she awoke and learned that he'd already explored Grandpa's farm. That he—*Leo*—had already had an adventure.

"I'll come," he declared, feeling uncharacteristically brave. "Oh, but should I change first?" He gestured to his pajamas, which were comfy but not ideal for adventuring.

Grandpa muttered something about city kids, then opened the door and stomped out onto the porch.

Leo took that as a no. He slipped his bare feet into his sneakers and followed, wondering what exactly he'd gotten himself into.

Grandpa's farm looked nothing like Applewood Acres.

Applewood Acres had orderly rows of squash and tomatoes and cucumbers, which Leo and Santos had planted and watered faithfully. It had neat red barns full of cows, pigs and chickens, which they'd raised, fed and protected from marauding wild pigs. It also had an orchard, an apiary and even a big pond for ducks and geese.

Grandpa's farm, on the other hand, had an overgrown field surrounded by a drooping barbed-wire fence, some rusty pieces of equipment that clearly hadn't moved in years and a very old barn with a roof that looked like it might cave in. When Dad saw the barn, Leo knew, he'd forbid him and Lizzie from going anywhere near it.

"Grandpa," Leo puffed as he hurried after him, past the barn and into the field behind it. Tall grasses brushed his bare arms and dew soaked through his sneakers, and he wished he'd brought his jacket. At home in Toronto, July mornings were often sticky-hot, but here on Heron Island, the air was much cooler.

"Hmm." Grandpa didn't look back or slow down.

"Um . . . what kind of crops do you grow?"

"Crops?" Grandpa repeated, like he'd never heard of them.

"Like tomatoes and squash. Do you grow vegetables?"

Grandpa shook his head. "Not anymore."

"Oh. Do you have any animals then?" Leo asked. "Like cows or pigs or goats?"

"Got rid of 'em ages ago," Grandpa replied. "Too much work, not enough time." He marched on, with *Everything Bees* tucked under his arm.

"Oh." Leo glanced around the farm with no crops and no animals. "So, um, what do you do here then?"

Grandpa stopped and looked back. "Do you ever stop questioning?" He sounded impatient.

Leo paused, unsure how to answer. He hadn't asked even *half* the questions that were piling up inside his brain! And trying to keep questions inside was a bit like trying to ignore the urge to pee: difficult if not impossible.

This, Dad had recently told him, was because he was an Auditor—at least according to Fatefinder.com, a website with personality quizzes that helped people find the jobs that best suited them. Dad was very into Fatefinder.com. Leo was very tired of hearing about it.

"It's in your nature to be curious and ask a lot of questions," Dad had explained. "But you have to try to be selective, Leo. Ask one question—*maybe* two if the person you're asking is patient."

Since patience didn't appear to be Grandpa's strong suit, Leo chose one question. "So what exactly are we doing?" he asked, hurrying after Grandpa.

"Telling the bees," Grandpa said again.

"Right. But . . . about what?" That was a second question, but it was necessary.

For a moment, Grandpa didn't answer. Finally, he said, "Evelyn."

"Eve— Wait, what?" Leo ground to a halt. "We're telling the bees about *Grandma? Why?*"

Grandpa stopped and turned around again. "Because it's what you do! The book says so." He held up *Everything Bees*, then spun on his heel and marched on.

"The book? But . . . wait!" Leo ran after him, his brain now bursting with questions.

Did the bees not know about Grandma?

Who had been taking care of them since she died?

What exactly was Grandpa going to tell them?

Did bees even understand English?

Grandpa halted where the field met the forest, and Leo stopped a few feet behind him. He recognized the beehives right away—they looked just like the hives in Applewood Acres: white boxes neatly stacked on wooden platforms. Inside each hive, he knew, was a colony made up of the queen bee, the worker bees and the drones. Depending on the time of year, each colony could contain up to 60,000 bees, which meant that Grandpa, with twelve hives, could have up to 720,000 bees!

Leo shivered, hoping they wouldn't have to get too close.

Grandpa opened his book and thumbed through a few pages. "Doesn't give much instruction," he muttered.

"What . . . does it say?" Leo inched forward.

Grandpa slammed the book shut and Leo jumped back.

"I'll just have to wing it," he said, then jabbed his index finger in Leo's direction. "*No* pun intended!"

Leo flinched. "Okay."

Grandpa turned to face the hives, paused a moment, then shouted, "She's gone!"

Leo gasped.

"She . . . she passed away," Grandpa went on, a bit quieter. "Back in February. Sorry for the late notice. I . . . only just read Chapter 6."

"What's in Chapter 6?" Leo whispered.

"When a beekeeper passes away, someone has to tell their bees what happened. I don't know why," Grandpa snapped before Leo could ask. "It's just what beekeepers *do*. Okay?"

"Okay," Leo said, though he had more questions. He was trying to decide which one to ask next when he heard someone calling his name. He squinted at the house and could just make out Dad standing on the back porch.

"What are you two doing out there?" Dad shouted.

"Nothing!" Grandpa hollered back. "He wouldn't understand," he grumbled to Leo.

Leo thought this was a huge understatement. If Dad knew that Grandpa was shouting to the bees about Grandma's death, he'd think Grandpa had lost his mind.

"Leo?" Dad yelled. "You're not still in your pj's, are you? I'll bring you a jacket!"

Grandpa sighed and shook his head.

"I can go back," Leo offered, half hoping Grandpa would say no, that it was important for Leo to take part in this mission, however strange it was. But Grandpa only nodded and turned back to the bees, leaving Leo with nothing to do but head back to the house, his sneakers soaking wet and his brain buzzing with questions.

No pun intended.

CHAPTER 2

Lizzie peered into the box of shredded wheat and wrinkled her nose. "*This* is breakfast?"

"This is breakfast." Mom pulled a carton of milk out of the fridge, opened it and sniffed. "Oh good, it hasn't gone off." She plunked the milk down on the table and gave Lizzie a smile that was half encouragement, half warning. "Just eat a bit, okay?"

"It's not that bad." Dad poked at the dry cereal in his bowl. "Only a little stale."

Lizzie grimaced, and Leo added breakfast to the list of things he missed about home, along with the soft carpet and the internet. At home, everyone ate what they wanted for breakfast. Leo made himself two slices of buttered toast sprinkled with cinnamon and as much sugar as Dad would allow, which wasn't much. Lizzie ate a peanut butter and strawberry jam sandwich, cut into quarters. Mom rarely had time for breakfast, but she'd tuck a banana and a granola bar into her briefcase on her way to the subway. And Dad would have plain soy yogurt.

Leo had always thought that plain soy yogurt was the saddest breakfast in existence . . . until he tried the shredded wheat from Grandpa's cupboard. It had probably been there for years. Maybe even decades.

"Tastes a bit like paper," Lizzie said, her mouth full of cereal. "But not the good kind."

"There's a good kind?" asked Leo, who was not surprised that Lizzie had a) eaten paper and b) had a preferred kind. Dad liked to say that she had an "adventurous palate," which really meant that she would eat anything once, even if it wasn't technically edible.

Mom shushed them and looked at the door, as if she expected Grandpa to stomp through it at any moment. He had yet to return from talking to the bees, and part of Leo wished he'd stayed to see what, if anything, had happened. He hadn't mentioned their strange mission to Mom, Dad and Lizzie; he'd simply said he'd gone with Grandpa to inspect the beehives. Lizzie hadn't been nearly as impressed as he'd hoped.

"I'll go to the grocery store this morning and get some food for the week," said Mom.

"Can you get peanut butter?" asked Lizzie. "And strawberry jam. And some bread."

Mom grabbed a piece of paper and pen from the counter and handed them to her. "Make a list, okay?"

"There's definitely no soy milk?" Dad asked for the second time.

"Just cow," Mom confirmed. "And don't ask him," she added. "You know how that will go."

"Okay, okay," Dad muttered to his dry cereal.

The back door swung open, and Grandpa tromped in. "Morning," he said. He hung up his crumpled hat, then picked his mug up off the table and took a swig of cold coffee.

"Hi, Dad." Mom smiled at him. "Hope you don't mind that we helped ourselves to cereal. Join us?" She patted the empty chair beside her.

"I don't eat breakfast," he informed her. But he sat anyway, raising an eyebrow at Dad's dry cereal.

A stiff silence fell over the table, and Leo added noise to the list of things he missed. At home, he could always hear the streetcars clanging down the tracks below their condo and the constant chirp of traffic lights, assuring pedestrians it was safe to cross the intersection. These were everywhere, all-the-time sounds. Sometimes they could even drown out the sound of Lizzie chewing.

Grandpa's house was so quiet Leo could hear a clock ticking at the other end of the house. Lizzie's mouth noises were deafening.

"The new fridge looks good," Mom commented.

Grandpa took a loud slurp of coffee, and Leo wondered if mouth noises could be a genetic trait, like the dark brown hair and eyes he'd inherited from Mom

(Lizzie had gotten Dad's sandy brown hair and blue eyes). "That fridge has been there for ages," Grandpa told her. "You'd know that if you visited more often. Or stayed longer when you did."

Mom pursed her lips. Dad sucked air through his teeth.

"Cookies!" Lizzie jabbed the air with her pen, then added it to her list.

Leo shook his head. Even when conflict was right in front of her, Lizzie almost never noticed it.

According to Dad (or rather, according to Fatefinder.com), this was because Lizzie was an Adventurer. Adventurers had the ability to tune out whatever didn't serve them in the moment so they could focus on fun and exciting things, like jumping out of an airplane or taming a tiger. Or in Lizzie's case, making a grocery list.

Leo couldn't imagine what that was like—he'd been aware of the tension between Mom, Dad and Grandpa since Mom had flown to Heron Island for Grandma's funeral back in February. He hadn't understood it at first, but thanks to some persistent questioning and a little eavesdropping, he'd figured out three important things.

The first was that Grandpa wasn't a big fan of Dad.

"You're just very different people," Leo had heard Mom tell Grandpa on the phone one night, back in June. He'd been sitting at the kitchen table, pretending to do his math homework but actually eavesdropping. Lizzie had been there too, but she'd been watching a Pandora Ali video and was oblivious to conflict, as usual.

"Alex doesn't hate the outdoors, Dad," Mom had said into the phone. "He just . . . likes the indoors."

"I'm allergic to grasses," Dad piped up from the couch, where he was re-reading his Fatefinder.com personality profile, highlighting the parts he liked best. "And some trees. And animal dander. Remind him of that: I don't hate the outdoors, I'm just allergic to it."

Mom gave him a look that said she would not be relaying that message.

The second thing Leo had figured out was that although it had been twenty-five years since Mom had left Heron Island for Toronto, Grandpa was still upset that she'd never moved back. This seemed rather unfair since Mom had an important job at a hospital charity and couldn't exactly pack up and move across the country. And what would they all do on Heron Island, which was so small it didn't even have its own school? According to Mom, the island kids had to board a boat every weekday morning and travel across the deep, dark ocean to a bigger island for school. It sounded like the worst commute on Earth—even worse than the subway in rush hour.

The third thing Leo had figured out was that Grandpa thought Mom should visit more often and stay longer when she came. This was more understandable, considering Leo had only been to Heron Island one other time, when he was three and Lizzie was just a baby. But Mom rarely got more than a week off work at a time, and she always said that wasn't long enough for a visit.

Grandpa was especially upset because when Mom flew to Heron Island for Grandma's funeral, she'd only stayed for five days, and she hadn't brought Dad, Leo or Lizzie with her.

Now Mom swallowed her shredded wheat as if it were a large, jagged rock. "Dad, we've been over this. I wanted to stay longer, but I couldn't. Work was crazy, and the kids were in school." She took a deep breath and let it out slowly. Had they been at home, Leo knew, she would have been filling her aromatherapy diffuser with lavender oil. She always did that when she was stressed.

When Grandpa didn't answer, Mom turned to Leo and Lizzie and forced a smile. "So what should we do today? Maybe we could go to the pizza place in town for lunch?"

"Pizza!" Lizzie cheered.

"That place closed down three years ago," Grandpa grunted. "You'd know that if you visited more often and stayed—"

"Oh, come *on!*" Mom slammed down her spoon. She stood up and marched out of the kitchen.

Silence descended again, and Leo added Mom's aromatherapy to the list of things he missed. Aromatherapy, of all things.

Grandpa grumble-huffed to his cold coffee.

"Hey!" Lizzie looked up from her grocery list. "Are there any cats around here?"

"Sure are," said Grandpa. "In the barn. Kittens too, last time I checked."

"Kittens!" Lizzie gasped, dropping her pen.

Leo stole a glance at Dad, wondering if he'd seen the barn with its dodgy-looking roof. But Dad stayed quiet, stirring his dry cereal with his spoon. Clearly he hadn't.

"Can I go?" Lizzie begged. "Right now?"

"They aren't pets, you know," Grandpa warned. "They're feral."

"What does that mean?" she asked.

"Wild," Grandpa answered at the same time Dad said, "Possibly diseased. Definitely not vaccinated."

Grandpa gave him a long look, then shook his head.

"Wild!" Lizzie whispered, and Leo knew she was thinking about Pandora Ali, her favorite YouTube star. Pandora Ali was a professional cat rescuer who traveled the world with her Bengal cat, Artemis. She piloted her own helicopter and would swoop down to rescue kittens from high-rise rooftops and pull mountain lions from raging rivers. Once she and Artemis even helped find a tiger that escaped from a zoo in Madrid. That video had six million views on YouTube, at least half of which, Leo was certain, were Lizzie's.

Mom stepped back into the kitchen, smelling like lavender aromatherapy oil. "You can go," she said. "But be careful, okay? And don't touch the kittens."

Leo rolled his eyes. Telling Lizzie not to touch a kitten was like telling a bee to stay away from a flower. Pretty well useless.

"Leo, you'll go with her, right?"

He nodded—he knew the drill—and stood up from the table.

"That's our Auditor." Dad grinned at him. Leo cringed.

Grandpa looked at Dad in disbelief. "Did you just call him an *auditor*?"

Dad nodded. "I don't suppose you've heard of Fatefinder.com?"

"Maybe this isn't the time." Mom rubbed her temples.

"Come on, Leo, let's go!" Lizzie cried, and for once Leo was thankful that she could be completely oblivious to conflict. He abandoned his soggy cereal and beelined for the door.

CHAPTER 3

"The roof looks weird," Lizzie observed when she saw the barn. Then she shrugged and marched right in.

Adventurers. Leo shook his head.

He hung back to assess the situation. A light breeze was tousling the tall grass in the field, but it didn't seem strong enough to make the roof collapse. He looked for signs of an approaching storm, but the sky was blue, almost cloudless. That didn't make it entirely safe, of course. An earthquake could occur at any moment—Leo had read that earthquakes weren't uncommon on the West Coast.

He weighed these risks against his promise to keep an eye on Lizzie—and, of course, the prospect of seeing the kittens. He wasn't a cat fanatic like his sister, but he did want to see them. Slowly and carefully, he followed her through the open barn door, then stopped to let his eyes adjust to the darkness. The barn smelled old and musty, and it occurred to him that he'd never considered what the barns in *Applewood Acres* smelled like, though he'd spent so much time in them feeding the animals and cleaning up their messes.

He found a light switch on the wall and flicked it, illuminating a bare bulb overhead. There were six animal stalls: three on his right and three on his left. Lizzie was wandering down the aisle between them making soft chirping noises like Pandora Ali did when she was approaching a wild or injured cat.

She stopped at the last stall on the right. "Leo!" she whispered. "They're here!"

He hurried over and peered inside. Sure enough, five kittens were playing on a bed of straw: two black ones, a gray tabby, a white one with black spots and a completely white one. Next to them lay a big tabby cat who was clearly the mom.

"They're adorable!" Lizzie slipped into the stall. The kittens froze and stared up at her.

"Careful, they're feral," Leo reminded her. "That means—"

"I know, I know." Still chirping softly, she lowered herself to the floor. The two black kittens ducked behind the mom cat, but the others stayed put, eyeing her cautiously. "We'll let them get used to us," she whispered. "Remember when Pandora Ali found the injured ocelot that was stuck on the edge of a cliff? She camped there for two days before it let her get close." She settled down on the straw. "We might be here a while."

Leo sighed. He had no desire to spend two days on the cold floor of a dark barn, but neither did he want to go back to the house and listen to Mom, Dad and Grandpa argue, or worse, discuss Fatefinder.com.

Would Grandpa agree that he was the family Auditor, as Dad liked to say? Leo wondered. Would he even know what that meant? Leo hadn't known himself until a few months back, when Dad had made him, Lizzie and Mom take a Fatefinder personality quiz. He'd shared their results over dinner, starting with Leo, the Auditor.

"A tax auditor reviews financial records," Mom had explained when Leo asked what an auditor did. "Auditors come to our office every year to look at our tax records and make sure we're filing things correctly."

Leo blinked at her. "That's it?"

Lizzie laughed. "That's so boring!"

Dad shushed her, then continued reading Leo's profile. "'Auditors are careful people, reluctant to take risks and always aware of the consequences of their actions. They think hard before they act, envisioning everything that can possibly go wrong.'"

"That's true, Leo. You do that." Lizzie nudged him.

He glared at her.

Dad read on: "'Auditors don't seek out excitement, preferring armchair adventures to real-life experiences.' That means you'd rather read about or watch other people's adventures than have your own," he told Leo.

"That's true too," Lizzie put in. "All your adventures are actually video games."

Leo opened his mouth to argue, then shut it because she was right. His ears burned.

"'Auditors are the most responsible people you'll meet,'" Dad concluded. "'They're well suited to be accountants, bookkeepers and actuaries.'"

"What's an actuary?" Leo asked, praying it was more interesting than an accountant.

"Someone who assesses risk," Mom said, sounding tired.

Lizzie pretended to snore. Leo set down his fork.

"It's just an online quiz, Leo," Mom assured him.

"But a very accurate one," said Dad, who'd been taking a lot of quizzes since he'd quit his job managing a computer repair shop. Fatefinder.com was his favorite—he was certain it would help him find a new career path.

"Read mine!" Lizzie commanded, slurping her spaghetti.

"You're the Adventurer," Dad told her. "'You're always open to new experiences and you love meeting new people. You're a risk-taker with an amazing ability to tune out what doesn't serve you in the moment so you can focus on what's fun and exciting.' See?" he said to Mom. "That's accurate."

He continued: "'You're best suited to a career as a film director, a travel guide or a pilot. But you're so adaptable you could probably excel at anything, as long as it doesn't involve sitting at a desk.'"

Leo groaned.

"Maybe let's talk about something else," Mom suggested,

topping up her wineglass.

"Don't you want to know yours? You got the Counselor," Dad went on. "'You're caring, a good listener and wise. People always confide in you.' That's true, isn't it?"

"Uh-huh," said Mom. She'd recently been promoted to Director of Human Resources at the hospital charity, and as Leo understood it, she spent most of her days listening to people's problems and trying to fix them.

"You could be a therapist, a teacher or a spy," said Dad.

"A spy!" cried Lizzie.

"That's so cool," Leo moaned. Why couldn't he be the Counselor?

Mom went to fill the aromatherapy diffuser with lavender oil.

Dad had gotten the Problem Solver—that meant he was good at not only finding problems but coming up with solutions. "I'm practical, but also creative," he told Leo and Lizzie, sounding pleased. "I'd make a great engineer, architect or software developer. I sure like the sound of software development!"

He printed out all four profiles and stuck them on the fridge so everyone could consider their career options when they went to get a snack.

It never failed to make Leo lose his appetite.

The gray tabby kitten had mustered the courage to creep up to Lizzie and sniff her outstretched hand. It paused, looked back at its mom, then walked right onto Lizzie's lap.

"Leo!" she whispered.

He nodded. Of course she'd managed to tame a wild kitten. *Of course.*

"Let's keep this one," she said as the kitten began to play with the zipper on her hoodie. "No, let's keep all of them."

"Dad's allergic," Leo reminded her. He'd given up asking for a pet years ago.

"Hello?" someone called, startling them all. The kitten leaped off Lizzie's lap and zipped back to its mom. "Is someone in there?"

"We are!" Lizzie called back.

"Lizzie!" Leo scolded.

"What? We are."

"You don't know who it is!" He stood up and peered out of the stall. A short, dark-haired woman wearing jeans and work boots stood in the doorway.

"Oh, hi!" She waved. "You must be Sarah's kids!"

She looked friendly enough, and she knew Mom's name, so Leo nodded.

The woman smiled and stepped inside. "I'm Béatriz. Your grandma was a friend of mine. Your mom was too, a long time ago."

"Hi!" Lizzie hopped out of the stall. "I'm Lizzie, and this is Leo."

"Nice to meet you both." Béatriz smiled. "I was just on my way to see the bees. I've been helping Sam take care of them since Evelyn passed away."

"You're a beekeeper?" asked Leo.

Béatriz nodded.

"Leo's a beekeeper too." Lizzie elbowed him. "But only virtually."

"Lizzie!" He shot her a death glare, which she ignored.

"Want to see the wild kitten I just tamed?" she asked Béatriz.

"Of course!" Béatriz followed them to the stall and watched as Lizzie demonstrated how, if you stayed very still and quiet, the kittens would eventually get used to you and approach. "We're going to keep at least one of them," Lizzie said as the tabby kitten crept back into her lap, this time followed by the two black ones.

"We can't keep any," Leo informed her. "Our dad's allergic."

Béatriz winked at him, and they watched as Lizzie picked up a black kitten and cradled it in her arms. Leo held his breath, waiting for the kitten to swipe at her with its tiny but deadly claws. But the kitten just blinked up at Lizzie, then began to purr.

"That's impressive," said Béatriz. "You must have a way with animals."

Lizzie nodded happily, and Leo had a vision of her as an adult, hopping out of her helicopter and striding across the tarmac with a pet leopard at her side. Excelling at everything she did, as long as it didn't involve sitting at a desk.

And he would be stuck in an office, going through someone's tax documents, making sure they'd filed everything correctly.

It was just too depressing for words.

CHAPTER 4

Later that afternoon, Leo was sitting at the kitchen table when Dad burst through the back door, his face flushed. "How can it be so hard to get an internet signal around here?" he demanded.

"At least your phone has data," grumbled Leo, who'd resorted to playing the only game on his phone that didn't require a Wi-Fi connection. It involved identifying every country on a map of the world, which meant it wasn't so much a game as geography homework. It made him very grumpy.

"I had to stand in the middle of the field and wave my phone at the sky for ten minutes before I got a signal!" Dad pulled a tissue out of his pocket and wiped his nose. "And with all the grasses out there, I couldn't stop sneezing."

Leo hoped Grandpa hadn't seen this.

"Anyway, it finally worked." Dad plopped down on a chair beside him. "And I've got some incredible news."

"Did you get a job?" asked Leo. Following Fatefinder's advice, Dad had been applying for jobs in software development.

"Better." He grinned. "There's been a cancellation at the Porpoise Island Spa and Resort!"

"A what?" Leo looked up from his phone. "At the what?"

"It's a world-renowned spa on Porpoise Island, not far from here," Dad explained. "I tried to book it months ago, when we decided to take this trip. It was supposed to be a birthday gift for your mom. But the resort was booked solid until December—it's that popular! They put my name on a wait list, though, and I just got an email: someone canceled a four-night stay, so we can go this week!"

Leo put down his phone. "We're going to a spa and resort?" He didn't care about the spa, of course, but a resort would definitely have Wi-Fi. And a swimming pool—maybe with a waterslide? Even if it didn't, it would be better than staying on a farm that wasn't really a farm, watching Lizzie tame wild kittens and listening to Mom, Dad and Grandpa argue. "When do we leave?" he asked.

Before Dad could answer, Lizzie marched through the back door, letting it bang shut behind her. "Is there any juice around here?" she demanded. Without waiting for an answer, she opened the fridge and stuck her head inside.

"Lizzie!" Leo exclaimed. "We're going to a resort!"

"Well, I haven't actually booked it yet," said Dad.

"Huh?" Lizzie backed out of the fridge. "We are?"

"For four nights!" Leo could barely contain his excitement.

She frowned. "But what about the kittens? I want to stay with them."

"Lizzie, it'll have Wi-Fi," Leo told her. "And a pool with a waterslide!" he added, though he didn't know if that was true.

"Keep your voices down, okay?" said Dad. "I haven't told—"

"What about Grandpa?" said Lizzie.

"What about me?" Grandpa asked, striding into the kitchen.

"Oh, hey, Sam." Dad straightened in his chair. "It's, uh, nothing. We were just—"

"We have to go to a resort," Lizzie lamented. "And I don't want to. I'd rather stay here with the kittens."

"Lizzie!" Leo groaned.

"A resort!" Grandpa put his hands on his hips. "Where? When?"

Dad swallowed. "Well, we'd be leaving tomorrow if—"

"*Tomorrow*?" Grandpa repeated. "But you just got here!"

"I know, Sam, but—"

The back door opened once more, and this time Mom stepped through carrying an armload of groceries.

"Mom, I don't want to go to the resort!" cried Lizzie.

"Well, I do!" Leo declared.

"This is ridiculous," Grandpa huffed.

"Everyone, calm down." Mom took a deep breath and turned to Dad. "Alex, what's going on?"

Dad hopped out of his chair and took the grocery bags from her arms. "I just got a message from the Porpoise Island Spa and Resort," he explained. "They had a last-minute cancellation and offered us a four-night stay. I didn't say yes, of course. But maybe we want to consider it?" He set a bag down on the table, and Lizzie immediately stuck her head inside.

"Oh, Alex." Mom sighed. "We can't."

"No kidding," Grandpa grumbled.

"I know it's a sudden change of plans," said Dad. "But this is the *Porpoise Island Spa and Resort*. There's no talking allowed in the spa, remember? You love a spa where people aren't allowed to talk."

"You could just stay here and not talk," Grandpa suggested.

"I'm pretty sure kids aren't allowed in the spa either," Mom pointed out.

"What about kittens?" Lizzie grabbed a juice box out of the bag.

"Of course not!" Leo exclaimed.

"Then what's the point?" She stabbed a straw into her juice box and sucked on it noisily.

"Look, it's a nice idea, but it's not going to work," Mom said.

"What if Sam came too?" Dad persisted. "He could watch the kids during the day."

"If you think I'm going to the Porpoise Island Spa and Resort, you're out of your mind!" cried Grandpa. "I wouldn't set foot in that place if they paid me. It's an abomination!"

"It is?" Lizzie stopped slurping. "What's that?"

"It's . . . it's something very bad," Grandpa sniffed.

"Wow. We'd better stay here then," said Lizzie. "With the kittens."

"Oh, come on!" Leo threw his hands in the air.

"Well, I'm definitely staying here," said Grandpa.

"And we are too," added Mom.

Leo slumped in his chair, deflated.

"All right, all right." Dad sighed. "I just thought it would be good for you. You need a break after all you've been through this year, Sarah. You know you do." He gave Mom a meaningful look. She shrugged and continued unloading the groceries.

Leo knew what he meant. Back in January, Mom had gotten her big promotion at work, which seemed like a great thing until she learned her first task was to lay off thirty-six people. This meant she had to sit down with each one of them and tell them they'd lost their jobs. Many of them were her friends. Most of them had cried.

Then a month later, Grandma had passed away. No one saw it coming, not even Mom, who'd talked with her on the phone hours before it happened. They'd chatted about normal things, like Grandma's beehives and Lizzie's science fair project on cat behavior. Then

Grandma had said goodbye, gone to bed and just . . . didn't wake up. It was most likely a stroke, Mom had explained before she'd hopped on a plane and flown across the country to help Grandpa arrange the funeral. She could only stay for five days since her bosses needed her to deal with the people she'd laid off, many of whom were still quite upset.

Mom had gone through several bottles of lavender oil during the winter.

"We'll go to the spa another year," she told Dad. "I'll probably still need it," she added jokingly.

"It would have been boring anyway." Lizzie finished her juice box and smacked her lips. "Going to a spa isn't an adventure."

Mom ruffled her hair. "Well, not all of us want adventures. Right?" She winked at Leo.

Lizzie giggled. "Just armchair adventures."

Leo glared at her. Then he glared at Mom. It was bad enough that he'd just lost his one chance to have fun on this vacation. Now they had to remind him that he was the family Auditor? He folded his arms across his chest.

"That wasn't an insult," Mom said quickly. "I just meant that some people don't need their vacations to be adventurous. I'm definitely one of them."

"And so is Leo," Lizzie added.

"Would you stop?" he snapped. He let out a Grandpa-style grumble-huff, which felt surprisingly good. But no one seemed to notice.

Maybe it was the glare of the yellow walls. Or the scream of Grandpa's teakettle. Or the sound of Lizzie sucking on the straw although her juice box was clearly empty.

Whatever it was, it made Leo suddenly do something completely out of character. Something an Auditor would never, ever do.

"I think you two should go," he blurted.

"Huh?" said Lizzie.

"I'm sorry?" Mom looked up from the cartons of soy milk she was stacking on the table.

"You do?" asked Dad.

He did not. But he nodded, because it felt good to see them all looking so surprised. "Yes. You two should go, and Lizzie and I will stay with Grandpa. It'll be . . ." He swallowed. "An adventure."

Lizzie's mouth fell open. Her straw fell out.

"It's okay, Leo." Mom squeezed his shoulder. "We're not going."

He knew that. But there was a note of pity in her voice that made him persist. "No, I mean it, you should go. You love a good spa."

Lizzie picked her straw up off the floor and popped it back in her mouth. "Leo's right: you should go, and we'll stay here. It'll be fun."

Leo nodded, trying to look like someone who'd actually want that and not someone who thought it sounded horrendous.

34

"You know, that's not a bad idea," Dad said. "My parents used to leave me with my grandparents all the time."

"Your grandparents lived across the street from you," Mom reminded him.

And more importantly, Leo thought, Dad's grandparents liked him. He didn't say this aloud, though.

"Look, I appreciate this, but—" Mom began.

"I think Leo's right," Grandpa declared, making Leo jump. He'd forgotten Grandpa was even in the kitchen. They all turned to look at him.

"You should go," he said. "Have your spa vacation, if that's what you really need. The kids can stay here with me."

"YES!" Lizzie cheered.

"Really?" Mom looked shocked. "But Dad, we just got here. And you said—"

Grandpa waved her off. "The kids and I will have fun. It'll be an adventure. Right?" He looked at Leo.

Leo's mouth suddenly went dry. He turned back to Mom, willing her to ignore Grandpa.

Mom glanced between him and Grandpa. "You really think we should?"

"It would only be for four nights," Dad put in. "We'd still have a few days to spend here when we got back." He made it sound like a few days would be plenty. Grandpa grunted in agreement.

At this point, Leo began to panic. This was NOT how things were supposed to go. What if Mom and Dad actually did leave, and something awful happened while they were gone? What if he or Lizzie got stung by bees and turned out to be deathly allergic? What if the barn roof collapsed while they were inside it? Would Grandpa know what to do?

Questions filled his brain like water filling a sinking ship. He tried to choose just one: the question that would make Mom and Dad reconsider this crazy idea that he now deeply regretted suggesting.

"What . . . um, what will we eat?" he asked.

Mom frowned. "Good question. I didn't buy nearly enough food for four days." She turned to Grandpa. "And you don't cook, do you?"

Grandpa looked insulted. "I cook! I make sardines on toast every day."

"Ew." Lizzie grimaced. "Maybe we can just eat cookies."

"You can't live off cookies," Mom told her.

Leo sighed with relief. She would never leave them without food.

"I wonder if Béatriz might help out?" she mused. "She's an old friend of mine."

"We know," said Lizzie. "We met her."

"You did? When?"

"She'd bring us food?" Leo cut in impatiently. "Are you sure?"

"I'd have to ask," said Mom. "She might be too busy, but she is a fantastic cook. If I remember correctly, her lasagna is to die for."

"You love lasagna." Dad nudged Leo.

He did love lasagna. But he still had questions. "How do you know she'll bring it? Is she trustworthy?" It was an Auditor question, but he didn't care.

"Very," said Mom. "She's a doctor, you know."

"I haven't met her, but I've heard she's brilliant," Dad added. "I bet she'd be a Problem Solver on Fatefinder.com."

Mom took a deep breath. "But Leo." She looked him square in the eye. "Is this really what you want? We absolutely don't have to go."

It was not what he wanted. In fact, he couldn't think of anything he wanted less. But how could he say that now?

He looked away and nodded.

"Fine by me," said Grandpa.

Mom shook her head, mystified. "Well, okay then."

"Okay?" said Dad.

"It's better than okay," Lizzie cried. "It's an adventure!"

Grandpa picked up his mug of tea and *Everything Bees* and went to sit in the living room. Dad hurried off to call the Porpoise Island Spa and Resort. Lizzie helped herself to cookies and began to tell Mom about the kittens in the barn.

And Leo slipped away unnoticed. He headed for his room, where he could sit in silence and consider everything that could possibly go wrong and, worst of all, how he'd brought it on himself.

CHAPTER 5

For the rest of the day, Leo kept to himself, desperately hoping Mom and Dad would come to their senses and realize that no matter what Leo had said, leaving him and Lizzie with Grandpa so they could go to a spa was a terrible idea.

But Mom and Dad seemed to grow more excited as the day went on, especially after Mom talked to Béatriz, who immediately offered to whip up a batch of lasagna the very next day. By dinnertime, they were jabbering nonstop about the eucalyptus-scented steam rooms and Egyptian cotton robes that awaited them on Porpoise Island. Grandpa rolled his eyes so many times Leo thought he might injure his eyeballs.

That night, Leo could barely sleep thanks to all the questions in his brain and the knots in his stomach. By the time Mom and Dad were ready to leave the next morning, he felt like he was going to throw up.

"You're absolutely certain about this, Leo?" Mom crouched down to look him in the eye. They were standing on the front steps of the house. Dad was loading suitcases into the little, blue rental car.

Leo had never been so uncertain about anything in his life.

"We'll be fine." Lizzie slipped between them and gave Mom a hug. "We're going to have so much fun. Right, Leo?"

He swallowed and nodded.

Dad shut the trunk of the car, jogged up the steps and hugged both Leo and Lizzie at once. "You're going to have a great time," he said. "And with our Auditor in charge, what could go wrong?"

Leo couldn't believe it. Here he was, doing the most adventurous thing he'd ever done, and Dad was *still* calling him an Auditor?

Grandpa said goodbye and went back into the house, but Leo stayed on the front steps with Lizzie as Mom and Dad hopped into the car and buckled themselves in. He couldn't believe they were actually leaving. Nor could he believe how quickly Dad backed the car out of the driveway and peeled off down the road. Dad never drove over the speed limit.

"Bring us back a porpoise!" Lizzie shouted, though of course they couldn't hear her. Leo began to tell her so, but the dust the car left behind caught in his throat.

"Well, they're gone!" Lizzie declared, wiggling her eyebrows. "Adventure time!"

He gazed at the road, willing the car to reappear.

"You're going to be boring, aren't you?" She sighed. "Well, I'm going to the barn. I saw another kitten yesterday. She's a bit older than the others, and I think she's a Bengal cat like Artemis." She hopped down the steps, then paused and looked back. "You can come with me if you want."

He didn't, really. But he followed her to the barn because it was his job to keep an eye on her. And anyway, what else was he going to do?

Inside, he watched as she coaxed a young cat out of one of the stalls. It had watchful green eyes and brown spots on cream-colored fur. He could see why she thought it was a Bengal, though he was fairly certain it wasn't. Bengal cats were rare and expensive—Pandora Ali had apparently paid four thousand dollars for Artemis!

"You have to keep your eyes on the ground," Lizzie whispered as the kitten crept toward her. "Pandora Ali says that wild cats sometimes feel threatened or challenged when you look right at them."

"A lot of animals do," Leo told her. "In *Applewood Acres 3*, we had to avoid eye contact with the wild pigs. Otherwise they would attack."

She wrinkled her nose. "That's a video game. Not real life."

"So what?" he shot back. "You get all your cat facts from Pandora Ali. She's the one who has the adventures, not *you*."

She shrugged. "Maybe for now. But I *will* have adventures. Loads of them."

The most irritating thing was that Leo knew she was right.

Twenty minutes later, Lizzie had lured the kitten right into her lap.

"Maybe it has an owner," Leo suggested grumpily.

"Or maybe I'm just a really good cat tamer." Lizzie giggled as the cat reached up to bat her hair. "We're definitely keeping this one."

Leo shook his head but didn't argue. If Lizzie wanted to believe that, fine. Mom and Dad could set her straight when they got back from their stupid vacation.

Hours passed, and Grandpa didn't appear once—not to make sure the roof hadn't collapsed or even to ask if they were hungry. Leo wondered if they'd be left to fend for themselves for the next four days. Was this Grandpa's idea of fun? Or did he think that with an Auditor in charge, there was nothing to worry about?

Around midday, the sound of tires on gravel made him leap up from the floor. He dashed to the door, hoping to see the rental car returning and Mom and Dad tumbling out, full of remorse for leaving their kids behind.

Instead, he saw a dark green truck lurch to a halt in front of the house. The words "Jacques of All Trades" were painted in big, white letters on one side. Leo squinted and could just make out the driver: a middle-aged man wearing a cap the same color as his truck.

The passenger door opened and a boy hopped out, also wearing a green cap. He looked to be around Leo's age or maybe a bit younger. As Leo watched, the boy lifted a box off the truck bed, carried it to Grandpa's front steps and knocked on the door.

"Is that Béatriz?" Lizzie yelled from the stall.

"Uh-uh." Leo had no idea who this was.

The front door swung open and Grandpa poked his head out. Leo was too far away to hear their conversation, but even from a distance he could tell Grandpa wasn't pleased. The boy picked up the box, carried it back to the truck, then returned moments later with a big brown bag.

The driver tooted the truck's horn and the boy dropped the bag at Grandpa's feet, then ran back to the truck and hopped in. Before he'd even closed his door, the truck was reversing down the driveway, scattering gravel in all directions. Grandpa grabbed the bag and slammed the front door.

"What was that about?" Lizzie asked, appearing at Leo's side.

"No idea," he said.

"What do you think I should call her?"

"Huh?" Leo glanced at her. "Who?"

"My kitten, of course. I'm almost positive she's female."

He frowned. "Maybe don't name her." His time in *Applewood Acres* had taught him that you should never name the animals you'd eventually have to eat, and he imagined this rule also applied to animals you'd eventually have to leave behind. It was best not to get too attached.

"How about Lightning? She's superfast. Or Pounce?"

He shook his head. "I'm going to go find out what that kid left."

"I'll come too," said Lizzie. "Hopefully it's the lasagna."

They walked back to the house and let themselves into the kitchen, where they found Grandpa making coffee and muttering to himself. The big brown bag was sitting on the table, smelling unmistakably like lasagna.

"Help yourselves," Grandpa said. "I'm going out to check on the bees."

"Who delivered it?" asked Leo. "That wasn't Béatriz."

"She must have been too busy to come herself," Grandpa said. "That was a local guy, Jacques, who runs a delivery service. He also does odd jobs, like fixing fences and opening people's car doors when they lock their keys inside. You can pay Jacques to do pretty well anything—he just might not do it well."

Leo recalled the words painted on the side of Jacques's truck. "Oh, I get it! He's a jack-of-all-trades!"

Grandpa grunted to his coffeepot.

"What does that mean?" Lizzie opened the bag and peered inside. "Mmm, that smells so good."

"A jack-of-all-trades is someone who does a lot of different things," Leo explained. "That guy's name is Jacques, so he's a '*Jacques* of All Trades.' That's what it said on his truck."

"Why does he have to do so many different things?" Lizzie sat down at the table.

"Lots of people around here have more than one job," said Grandpa. "It's how they make ends meet."

"Did you have more than one job, Grandpa?" she asked.

"I was a farmer. That's a lot of jobs in one," he replied, sloshing coffee into his mug.

Leo nodded—he knew this from *Applewood Acres*. He considered telling Grandpa about it but knew Lizzie would point out that he'd only been a *virtual* farmer. So he kept quiet. Maybe he'd mention it another time, when she wasn't around.

Grandpa took his mug of coffee and headed for the door.

"What about Grandma?" Lizzie persisted. "Did she do more than one thing?"

He paused with his hand on the doorknob. "She did everything," he said quietly. Then he stomped out onto the porch and let the door slam behind him.

Lizzie shrugged and lifted a covered dish out of the bag and set it on the table. "Ooh, it's still warm."

Leo grabbed two plates and began to dish up the lasagna—moderate portions, since he wasn't sure how long it would have to last.

The lasagna was heavy on cheese and light on vegetables, just the way he liked it. In fact, it might have been the best lasagna he'd ever eaten. But it was hard to

44

enjoy with so many questions piling up in his brain. Like, why hadn't Béatriz delivered the food herself? Did this mean she wasn't as responsible as Mom had said? If she was too busy to deliver food, could they count on her in an emergency?

Lizzie, meanwhile, devoured her dinner while doodling kittens on an unopened envelope addressed to Grandpa.

Leo shook his head. Only his sister could draw kittens amid so much uncertainty.

Also, when had she learned to draw so well?

"Adventurers," he muttered to his lasagna. It just wasn't fair.

That evening, they were all sitting in the living room—Grandpa reading *Everything Bees*, Lizzie doodling kittens, Leo playing his dull geography game—when the phone rang, cutting through the silence and making everyone jump.

Grandpa reached it first. "Hello?" He paused, then said, "Uh-huh," with no enthusiasm at all. He nodded at Leo. "Your dad."

"About time," Leo grumbled, taking the phone from Grandpa. It was an old-fashioned rotary phone, which he'd only ever seen in a museum, and it took him a moment to figure out how to speak into it. "Hi, Dad," he said eventually.

"Hey, buddy, how's it going?" Dad sounded chipper.

"It's . . ." Leo tried to think of the words to describe life at Grandpa's: incredibly boring, potentially dangerous, unbearably quiet.

But he *was* the one who'd insisted they leave. He swallowed hard. "It's fine."

"Great!" said Dad. He began to tell him about the Porpoise Island Spa, which was just as relaxing and luxurious as he'd heard.

"Mom says she wants to live forever in the eucalyptus-scented steam room where talking isn't allowed." He chuckled.

Leo saw nothing funny about this.

"This really is what she needed, Leo," Dad concluded. "So what's new at Grandpa's?"

Before he could answer, Lizzie snatched the phone from his hand. "My turn!" she cried. "Dad, I found the cutest kitten today!"

"Hey, I wasn't finished!" Leo protested.

"She looks like Artemis," Lizzie went on, ignoring him. "You know, Pandora Ali's cat? And she's super smart. You'll love her." She paused for a moment. "Yeah, I know, I won't touch her." She looked at Leo and crossed her eyes.

"Lizzie, that's not—"

"Okay, gotta go, Dad. Bye!" She hung up before Leo could stop her, then grinned. "Sometimes it's best if they don't know."

"Lizzie!" cried Leo. "I wanted to talk to him!" But she was already skipping off to the kitchen. "You're the worst," he called after her, then looked over at Grandpa. His mouth was twisted, like he was trying not to smirk.

Leo stomped off to his room.

That night, Lizzie wanted to stay up late, but Grandpa insisted they go to bed at nine o'clock as Mom and Dad had instructed. Leo was relieved. The sooner he could fall sleep, the sooner it would be morning and the closer they'd be to Mom and Dad's return.

But when they switched off the light between their beds, he found himself wide awake, staring into a darkness that was just so incredibly *dark*. His bedroom at home was never so dark—there were always streetlights glowing and traffic lights blinking outside his window. At any time of night, he could peek through the blinds and know he wasn't the only person awake.

Lizzie began to snore, and with no noise to drown her out, her snores were practically thunderous. Leo turned on one side and covered his other ear with his pillow, but it didn't do much good. So he made up a game that involved matching the sounds of Lizzie's snores with the sounds of farm animals in *Applewood Acres*.

He'd just begun to drift off when he heard a noise that for once wasn't coming from his sister. It was a low rumble, like an approaching thunderstorm. Or a car engine.

He held his breath, wondering if it might be Mom and Dad returning. But after a minute or so, the noise faded away.

Leo sighed. Of course it wasn't Mom and Dad. They were probably fast asleep in their Egyptian cotton sheets.

He grumble-huffed to the deep, dark night, then turned on his side and covered his ear again. Somehow, eventually, he fell asleep.

CHAPTER 6

"Lizzie, would you *stop*?" Leo groaned the next morning at breakfast. The only thing worse than listening to her chew was seeing the cereal inside her mouth. "That's disgusting!"

She smacked her lips and grinned. He looked across the table at Grandpa, hoping for backup. But once again Grandpa was focused on *Everything Bees*. Leo could see he was now on Chapter 7, "Overwintering Bees."

"I know a bit about that," Leo said, then braced himself for a remark about his virtual adventures. But Lizzie was busy mushing her shredded wheat into a paste with her spoon.

"Do you." Grandpa slurped his coffee but didn't look up.

He nodded, recalling what he'd learned from *Applewood Acres 3: What's the Buzz?* "I know you have to move the hives someplace sunny and warm. If it gets really cold, you can wrap them in insulation. Also, you can't forget to feed them in early spring, when there's no pollen available." He and Santos had indeed forgotten, and their carelessness had cost them several hives. "I also know that in the fall, the worker bees kick the drones out of the hive. I think it's because the drones have nothing to do in the winter, and the rest of the brood can't afford to feed them when they're just hanging around, doing nothing."

"You don't say," Grandpa muttered, turning a page.

Leo nodded, feeling a tiny bit bolder. "Hey, Grandpa?"

"Yep."

"Are you . . . reading that book for the first time?"

"Three pages a day," Grandpa confirmed.

"That's going to take a while," Lizzie commented. "It's a huge book. Is it a thousand pages long?"

"I don't know," he said curtly.

"You could check," she suggested. "The pages should have numbers."

Grandpa pursed his lips and continued reading. Leo shot Lizzie a "stop talking" look. She retaliated by opening her mouth, exposing half-eaten cereal.

"Lizzie!"

Grandpa threw his hands up. "Would you two just—"

"Hello?"

They all turned to see Béatriz at the back door, peering in from the porch.

"Can't I just read my book in peace?" Grandpa griped.

Béatriz opened the door and stepped inside. Her cheeks were flushed, as if she'd been running. "I'm sorry to bother you all, but . . ."

"What?" Grandpa snapped. "What is it?"

"Well . . ." She blinked at him. "What happened to the bees?"

"What do you mean what happened to them?" said Grandpa. "What did you do?"

"Sam." Béatriz took a deep breath. "The bees are gone."

"*Gone?*" Leo repeated.

"*Gone!*" Grandpa leaped off his chair as if he'd just been stung in the behind. "You mean they swarmed? That happened once before, maybe three years ago. I can't remember what Evelyn did, but I'm sure it's in here." He began rifling through *Everything Bees*.

"I know about that!" Leo blurted. "My bees swarmed once when the hive got too big. Usually the queen goes with the swarm, and then a new queen—"

"Those were *virtual* bees," Lizzie cut in. "Not real life."

He threw his hands in the air. "Would you—"

"Excuse me!" Béatriz raised a hand to quiet them, then turned to Grandpa. "Sam, the *hives* are gone. All twelve of them. They've disappeared!"

Grandpa stared at her. Then he slammed the book shut, grabbed his hat and ran outside. Béatriz followed close behind.

"Let's go!" Lizzie jumped up and sprinted after them.

Leo shoved his feet into his sneakers and grabbed a pair for Lizzie, who'd bounded out the door barefoot and would surely regret that. He jogged down the path toward the barn, then out into the field, his brain bursting with questions. How could twelve hives just disappear? Had someone borrowed them? Or stolen them? Did people *do* that?

He caught up with Grandpa, Béatriz and Lizzie at the edge of the field—the exact spot where Grandpa had told the bees about Grandma just two days before. Sure enough, the hives were gone. Only their wooden platforms remained, plus a few stray bees flying in circles overhead.

For a moment, they all stood open-mouthed, watching the bees loop lazily above them. Then Grandpa broke the silence with a big, fat curse word—one of the worst words Leo knew. Lizzie gasped in delight.

Grandpa shook his fists and roared at the sky. He stamped his foot and swore some more. He pulled off his hat and threw it on the ground.

"Leo and Lizzie, can you go finish your breakfast?" Béatriz asked quietly. "I'll deal with him." She nodded at Grandpa, who was now stomping on his hat, snorting like one of the wild pigs in *Applewood Acres 2: Hog Wild*.

"Grandpa—" Lizzie took a step toward him, but Leo grabbed her arm and pulled her back. "I want to stay and watch!" she protested.

"We'll watch from inside," he said, ushering her back to the house.

When they reached the kitchen, they climbed onto the counter and peered out the window over the sink. Leo could see Béatriz's curly hair bobbing and Grandpa's hands waving in the air.

"What's going on?" asked Lizzie.

"I think she's trying to calm him down," said Leo. "But it doesn't seem to be working."

After a while, Béatriz seemed to give up. They watched her hurry back to the house, jump into her Jeep and drive away, leaving clouds of dust in the driveway and Grandpa alone in the field. He sat down on the ground and disappeared in the long grass.

"Should we go check on him?" Lizzie asked.

Leo wasn't sure. "He might get upset."

"He's already upset," she pointed out.

He squinted out at the field, wondering how long Grandpa would stay out there. Would they have to bring him food?

Lizzie opened the fridge and helped herself to a juice box. "What do you think happened to the bees?"

Leo shrugged. Judging by Grandpa's reaction, it seemed unlikely that someone had borrowed them. But did people really go around stealing bees?

"I think we should call Mom and Dad," he decided. At the very least, they could contact the Heron Island police— if there were, in fact, police on Heron Island. He wasn't sure about that. But Mom would know. And when she heard about the stolen bees, she'd probably come straight back to help.

Heartened by that thought, Leo hurried for the phone in the living room. But just as he picked up the receiver, he heard a knock on the front door.

"I'll get it!" Lizzie dashed past him. "Maybe it's Béatriz. Ooh, maybe she brought more lasagna!"

"Lizzie, wait," Leo began, but it was too late. She opened the front door, then yelped.

"Whoa!"

"Oh no!" He dropped the receiver, suddenly realizing how dangerous, how completely *stupid* it was to answer the door after a potential incident of bee theft. Supposing the thieves had returned to pillage the house? Supposing they were armed and dangerous? He ran for the door, wishing he'd stopped her before she'd acted without thinking—again!

He froze when he saw them: not one, but *four* adults, huddled in the doorway, peering down at Lizzie. They looked to be around Grandpa's age, with silver hair and sun-speckled skin. They wore overalls and rubber boots and floppy hats, and they reminded Leo, just a little, of life-sized garden gnomes.

"Who are *you*?" Lizzie demanded.

A woman in red rubber boots and a purple bonnet stepped forward, extending a hand for Lizzie to shake.

"We are the Bumblers," she told her. "And we're here to help."

CHAPTER 7

The Bumblers didn't ask permission. They marched into Grandpa's house and headed for the kitchen, leaving Leo and Lizzie standing at the door, open-mouthed.

"What's a Bumbler?" Lizzie whispered.

Leo had no idea. He hurried after the intruders, who were already pulling up chairs around the kitchen table. Since there weren't enough chairs for everyone, one of the Bumblers—a man with extremely long legs—hopped up on the countertop. Leo had a feeling they'd been in the kitchen before, and an even stronger feeling that Grandpa wouldn't want them there.

He cleared his throat, took a deep breath and asked the most important question of all the questions in his brain. "So, um, who are you?"

"The Heron Island Bumblers," said the man on the countertop. He reminded Leo of a long-legged bird. Like an ostrich or a stork.

"Apiarists, all of us!" said the woman with the red rubber boots, which she hadn't bothered to take off when she tromped inside.

"Api-what?" said Lizzie.

"Beekeepers," Leo told her.

"Very good," a man with long, white hair commended him. "I don't suppose you also know the hive five?" Leo shook his head, and the man raised his hand for a high five. When Leo reluctantly raised his own hand, the man began to wiggle his fingers and make buzzing noises. He spun in a circle, then slapped Leo's hand. "That's our club handshake. The *hive* five."

Now Leo was one hundred percent certain Grandpa wouldn't want the Bumblers in his kitchen. He prayed they'd leave before Grandpa came back in.

"We heard what happened to Evelyn's bees," the woman with the boots told Leo and Lizzie. "Béatriz phoned me straightaway."

"She did?" said Lizzie.

She nodded. "Béatriz is a Bumbler too. But she's an honorary member, since she's so busy these days."

"We're all busy," sniffed the man on the counter. "I work on the ferry," he told Leo.

"Yes, but Béatriz saves lives," said the woman in the boots. "Anyway, she phoned me straightaway, and I put an emergency call out to the group."

"We dropped everything," said a woman who appeared to be wearing a shower cap.

"It's just what we do," said the woman in the boots. "Now then. Who's going to go get Sam?"

The Bumblers looked at each other, then looked down at their feet.

"Rock, paper, scissors?" the man on the counter suggested.

Everyone agreed, and a lightning round of rock, paper, scissors ensued. The woman in the boots lost and trudged out the back door.

"Let's introduce ourselves while we wait," the man on the counter suggested. "That's Marguerite, our current club president." He pointed at the woman who'd just left. "And I'm Bruno. I was president four years ago, and three years before that."

"I'm Jin," said the man who'd shown Leo the hive five. "President five years ago."

"Willa!" The woman in the shower cap waved. "I haven't been president yet, but maybe next year."

Bruno and Jin exchanged a look that seemed to indicate it wasn't likely.

"I'm Lizzie," Lizzie offered before Leo could stop her. "And that's Leo."

"Oh, we know!" Bruno said, swinging his long legs.

Leo began to ask how they knew, but stopped himself. It didn't really matter. What *did* matter was what would happen when Marguerite returned to the kitchen with Grandpa. Leo pictured a volcano exploding, spewing curse words like lava.

"This reminds me of *Alice in Wonderland*," Lizzie observed. "You know, the Mad Hatter's tea party?"

"That's my favorite scene," Bruno told her.

She beamed. "Should we make tea?"

"I don't think so," Leo said just as the Bumblers chorused, "Yes, please!"

Lizzie skipped over to the kettle.

"Now remember, everyone," said Jin. "We're here for Evelyn. Sam will probably be awful—"

"He'll *definitely* be awful," Willa cut in. She glanced around the kitchen as if searching for places to hide.

"But we're doing this for Evelyn."

"You knew Grandma?" asked Leo.

"Of course. Evelyn was president of the Heron Island Bumblers three years in a row," said Bruno. "I'm sure you know that."

Leo hadn't known that. But before he could ask anything more, Bruno glanced out the window and announced, "He's coming!"

"Oh dear." Willa grasped her shower cap with both hands, as if bracing for a storm. Which was fitting because moments later Grandpa burst into the kitchen like a hurricane. "What are you people doing here?" he thundered. He scanned the room until he found Leo. "Why did you let them in?"

Leo threw his hands in the air. "It wasn't me!"

"Kettle's boiled!" called Lizzie.

Grandpa spun to look at her. "You're making *tea*?"

She nodded. "Can you pass me some mugs?" she asked Bruno, who hadn't moved from the counter.

Grandpa's eyes bulged. Leo gulped.

"Now, Sam." Marguerite sat back down at the table. "We came as soon as we could to help you." Grandpa opened his mouth to object. "You *do* need our help, Sam. You won't find all the answers in that book." She pointed to *Everything Bees*, which Grandpa was still carrying under his arm.

"Listen—" Grandpa began, but Marguerite raised a hand for silence.

"As the seventeenth and current club president, I hereby call this impromptu meeting of the Heron Island Bumblers to order! All in favor?"

"Aye!" the others chorused.

"Aye!" Lizzie added.

"Lizzie!" Leo hissed.

"First order of business—"

"I think you mean *buzz*-iness," Bruno piped up.

"Oh, here we go," Grandpa moaned.

"Precisely," said Marguerite. "First order of buzz-iness, and really the only order of buzz-iness, is finding the missing bees." She turned back to Grandpa. "Sam, have you alerted the police?"

He harrumphed. "I have not."

"They'll help you, Sam," said Jin.

"They're useless," he retorted.

The Bumblers exchanged knowing looks.

"All right then," Marguerite soldiered on. "What do we know about the bees' disappearance?"

Grandpa stared out the window and refused to answer, so the Bumblers looked to Leo.

"Me?" He swallowed. "Um. Well . . ."

"You leave him out of this," Grandpa snapped. "All we know is that Béatriz came over this morning and found that the bees had disappeared." He paused a moment. "Or so she said."

Marguerite frowned. "There's no reason to suspect Béatriz, Sam."

He shrugged and looked back out the window.

"I heard a car drive by late last night," Leo suddenly recalled. "Or maybe a truck. I can't remember what time it was."

Marguerite tapped her chin. "It could have been the thieves."

"Rustlers," said Bruno.

Willa shivered. "But who would do that?"

"Maybe it was a new beekeeper," Jin suggested. "Someone who wanted established hives so they didn't have to set them up themselves."

Bruno snapped his fingers. "A new-*bee*!"

"Good one," said Jin.

"But could a beginner steal a dozen hives?" Marguerite wondered. "I think only a professional could pull that off. This must have been the work of an experienced apiarist."

"We know all the apiarists on the island," Jin pointed out. "With the exception of Béatriz, we're all here."

"Mm-hmm." Grandpa folded his arms across his chest and narrowed his eyes.

"Maybe it was a beekeeper from Porpoise Island," Bruno suggested.

"Or even farther afield," said Willa. "You know, this reminds me of an article I read recently about some thieves in the States who were stealing bees to pollinate almond orchards. A hive heist, they called it."

"Almonds are a big business—I mean buzz-iness," said Bruno. "We don't have any operations like that on Heron Island."

"It's a good point, though," said Marguerite. "The thieves might have already left the island. Sam, did you call the ferries and tell them to look for stolen bees on board?"

Once again, Grandpa didn't answer.

Willa sighed. "He doesn't trust the ferries either."

"To be fair, no one trusts the ferries," said Jin. "They're almost never on time."

"Maybe it was an act of revenge," Bruno suggested. "Sam, have you done anything to offend anyone lately? I mean, beyond just being yourself."

"*Bee*-ing yourself!" said Jin.

Bruno buzzed approvingly.

Grandpa gave them a murderous look. "I think it's time for you all to leave."

"But the tea's ready!" Lizzie handed a steaming mug to Marguerite.

"Thank you, dear," she said, then turned back to Grandpa. "Sam, you have to let us help. Evelyn would have wanted it."

"Now, don't tell me what Evelyn—"

"I think we'll be great detectives," Jin cut in, spooning sugar into his mug. "Who's better suited to tracking down bees than we are?"

Bruno snapped his fingers again. "We'll be the MI Hive! Get it? Like the MI5 but—"

"The MI Hive!" Bruno and Jin slapped five and began to buzz.

"Uh-oh," Leo whispered as Grandpa flared his nostrils, once again reminding him of the wild pigs in *Applewood Acres 2: Hog Wild*. His hands curled into fists and his cheeks turned tomato red. He took a deep breath, then bellowed, "GET OUT!"

Bruno slid off the countertop. "Now Sam—"

"NOW!"

"All right, all right." The Bumblers abandoned their mugs and hurried for the door. "If you change your mind, we'll—" Marguerite began.

"NOT ON YOUR LIFE!" Grandpa declared. They were barely out the door before he slammed it shut behind them.

Then he spun to face Leo and Lizzie. "*Never* let them in again. Never let *anyone* in again! Got that?"

Before they could answer, he grabbed *Everything Bees* and stormed off.

CHAPTER 8

That afternoon, the sky grew dark and it began to drizzle. That quickly turned into a shower, which in turn became a downpour. Leo sat on the kitchen counter near the window, watching Grandpa stomp back and forth across the field, his crumpled hat dripping and his sweater soaked through.

"What's he doing now?" Lizzie asked from the table, where she was once again drawing kittens on Grandpa's unopened mail. The more she drew, the more she improved, which Leo found extremely irritating.

"Stomping," he replied.

"Are you going to try calling Mom and Dad again?"

He shrugged. Neither one was answering their phone, which meant they were probably lounging in the eucalyptus-scented steam room where talking wasn't allowed. How long could a person sit in a steam room? he wondered, picturing his parents turning into eucalyptus-scented prunes. He shuddered.

"I'm so bored," Lizzie complained. "When will the rain stop?"

"It rains a lot on the West Coast," Leo reminded her. "Sometimes days or weeks at a time." It was one of the reasons Mom had wanted to move away for university, along with being sick of living on a tiny island where everyone knew everything about her.

"When I got to Toronto," she'd once told Leo, "I knew I'd come to the right place. There were so many people to meet, classes to take, museums and galleries to explore. I remember standing on the subway platform in rush hour and knowing I'd found my forever home." She'd smiled at the memory, then added, "Grandma and Grandpa didn't get it—Heron Island is their forever home. They feel like they're a part of the island, and it's a part of them."

Leo had pondered this a long time. Was Toronto his forever home too? Or was there someplace else out there where he belonged? And how would he know if he found it?

He slid off the counter and sat down at the table, where Grandpa had left *Everything Bees*. He opened it and began to thumb through.

True to its name, the book really did seem to contain everything you'd want to know about bees. There was a chapter about the bee's life cycle and another about the roles within a hive. There were chapters on feeding bees, overwintering bees, treating bee diseases and collecting honey. He could see why Grandpa only read three pages a day—there was a *lot* of information to take in.

But as far as Leo could see, the book said nothing about what to do if all your hives went missing in the dead of night.

If Grandpa were a normal person with an internet connection, Leo could have researched it online. He could have found the article about the hive heist that Willa the Bumbler had mentioned. He could have even revisited his apiary in *Applewood Acres 3: What's the Buzz?* It might not have helped him solve the crime, but it would have been more fun than watching Grandpa stomp around in the rain.

"I can't take it anymore!" Lizzie slammed down her pencil, startling Leo out of his thoughts. "I'm going out to the barn. Are you coming?" She hopped up and grabbed her jacket.

Leo knew he ought to go with her, especially considering the barn's sagging roof and Lizzie's inability to assess risk. But he had no desire to watch her become the next Pandora Ali, excelling at everything she did. "I'll stay here."

She shrugged, zipped up her jacket and skipped out into the rain.

Once she was gone, Leo wandered into the living room, where he perused the bookshelves and found an old game of Monopoly covered in a layer of dust. He hoped they wouldn't get bored enough to play that—Lizzie was annoyingly good at Monopoly. Somehow, she always managed to buy Boardwalk and Park Place, and then everyone else had to sit there and watch her get rich.

He turned away, and his eyes fell upon a framed photo of Mom. She was standing on a beach wearing a raincoat the color of the walls in Grandma's kitchen. He picked up the photo and stared at it. There was something not quite right about it. Mom's straight, dark brown hair and round face looked normal, but her smile was different. It was wide and bright and toothy.

Then he realized: it wasn't a photo of Mom. It was a photo of Grandma, taken when she was around Mom's age.

And suddenly, he recalled the last time he'd seen Grandma in person, when she and Grandpa had come to Toronto for a visit. He'd just turned seven, and Lizzie was five. They'd mostly stayed in the condo since Grandpa didn't like crowds or streetcars or sticky-hot summer days. But one day, toward the end of their visit, Grandma had taken Leo to the aquarium downtown. It was an outing just for the two of them, she'd said.

Leo had two distinct memories from that day. The first was the giant slice of chocolate cake Grandma had bought him at the aquarium cafeteria. It was the biggest slice of cake he'd ever seen—probably the size of his seven-year-old head. And the second thing he remembered was Grandma's excitement. She exclaimed over everything they saw, from the smallest sandworms to the hammerhead sharks. Mom later explained that Grandma had a degree in biology and loved teaching people about nature. In fact, when Mom was little, Grandma had started a nature club for kids on Heron Island. Every Saturday morning, she'd take them to explore a forest or beach or bog. They'd return home at the end of the day with tree sap in their hair and sand in their socks.

"That kind of thing lights her up," Mom told him. And he thought that was a good description—all day at the aquarium, Grandma had been practically glowing.

How could someone so sunshiny have married someone so stormy? Leo wondered. He wished he could ask Mom—she knew a lot about people.

Leo put the photo back on the shelf. Then he went over to the ancient rotary telephone and dialed Mom's cell for the third time.

But once again, no one answered. He tried Dad's phone and got the same result.

Leo let out a Grandpa-style grumble-huff and slammed down the phone, noting how much more satisfying it was to hang up an old rotary phone than a cell phone.

Then he stomped back to the kitchen, grabbed his jacket and headed out into the rain to make sure the barn roof hadn't collapsed on his sister.

Around dinnertime, the rain stopped and a breeze picked up, scattering the clouds so the sun could just peek through. By that time, both he and Lizzie were starving, so Leo heated up another ration of lasagna while Lizzie went off to find Grandpa. They waited until he'd come inside, shed his soggy layers and joined them at the table before digging in.

Once again, Leo's brain was full of questions. Had Grandpa made a plan to find the bees? Had he alerted the police yet? And what would they do when they ran out of lasagna? Would Béatriz bring more food, or was she too busy?

Before he could decide which of these questions was most important, Lizzie turned to Grandpa. "So what are you going to do?" she demanded.

He raised an eyebrow.

"About the bees," said Lizzie. "Will you let the Bumbleheads help you find them?"

"Bumblers," Leo corrected her.

Grandpa grunted approvingly. "You're right, they are bumbleheads. That's exactly why I'm not letting them help."

"What about the police?" Leo asked.

"As a matter of fact, I already called them," said Grandpa. "And just as I thought, they were completely useless—more concerned about a few unpaid parking tickets than the disappearance of seven hundred thousand bees."

"Seven hundred *thousand*?" Lizzie gaped.

"Wait, did you say unpaid parking tickets?" asked Leo. "Can you actually park illegally on Heron Island?"

Grandpa waved this off. "Anyway, if I'm going to get those bees back, I'm obviously going to have to take matters into my own hands."

"Meaning . . ." Leo had a bad feeling about this.

"I'm going to track down those criminals myself," Grandpa declared.

"Go Grandpa!" Lizzie applauded.

Leo glared at her. There was absolutely nothing to cheer about. Just off the top of his head, he could think of a dozen things that could go wrong with this plan. Supposing Grandpa actually did find the criminals? Supposing those criminals had weapons? Supposing Grandpa said something to offend them? That wasn't just possible—it was extremely likely.

He drew a deep breath and tried not to sound panicked. "Are you sure that's a good idea, Grandpa?"

"Yes," said Grandpa. "I'm going to start searching the island first thing tomorrow morning." He paused. "No, tonight—I'll start tonight! The sun won't set for at least a few hours, and I've wasted enough time today bumbling around out there. NO pun intended!" he added, pointing his fork at them.

"We'll come with you!" Lizzie bounced in her chair.

"What? Lizzie, no!" Leo hissed.

"No, you'll have to stay . . . Hmm." Grandpa frowned, as if he'd just remembered they were children.

"We can stay by ourselves," Leo assured him. "We'll be fine."

"But I want to—ow!" Lizzie yelped as Leo elbowed her in the ribs. She elbowed him back.

Grandpa sighed. "I guess you'll have to come with me."

"Yesss!" Lizzie punched the air.

"Wait!" said Leo. "Maybe Lizzie and I should stay here just in case . . ." He thought fast. "In case the police find the bees and bring them back?"

"Leo!" Lizzie groaned.

Grandpa stood and took his plate to the sink. "I can't leave you here alone—you're too young. How old are you again?"

"Twelve," Leo said.

"He's lying. He just turned eleven," Lizzie said. "And I'm nine."

"Too young," said Grandpa.

Leo glared at Lizzie, who glared right back. "*You're* the one who wanted an adventure, Leo! That's what you *said*, remember?"

"I didn't say I *wanted* one," he retorted. But she was right that he *had* gotten them into this mess.

"But look, if you're going to come, you'll have to behave," Grandpa warned.

"We will," Lizzie promised. "We'll be so so SO good. Ooh, can I bring my kitten? The Bengal that looks like Artemis."

"It isn't a Bengal," Leo told her. "And absolutely not."

"Fine, sure," Grandpa said, pocketing his wallet. "But we'll have to leave soon. Like right now."

"Wait!" Leo made one last desperate attempt to stall the mission. "Maybe we should call Mom and Dad first."

Grandpa donned his crumpled hat. "I don't want to worry them. Don't you think your mom would worry?"

"Definitely," said Lizzie.

Leo agreed, but that was also the point.

"We'll call them when we get back," Grandpa promised, heading for the door.

Lizzie ran for the barn to collect her kitten, leaving Leo with no choice but to put on his sneakers and follow, cursing himself for insisting Mom and Dad leave them with Grandpa. It was by far the stupidest thing he'd ever done.

Grandpa hopped into an old, brown truck parked in the driveway, and Leo reluctantly took the passenger seat. It smelled like mold, so he rolled down a window. Lizzie arrived a few minutes later with the kitten tucked in her hoodie. Its spotted head stuck out below her chin, green eyes bright and curious.

"This is so exciting!" She climbed over Leo and took the middle seat between him and Grandpa.

Leo crossed his arms and glowered.

Grandpa started the engine, then quickly shut it off. "I forgot one thing."

"What?" Leo sat up straight, hoping it was something important. Something that would mean they couldn't leave until the next day, which would buy him time to get a hold of Mom and Dad and demand they come back.

"I have one rule, and you absolutely have to follow it." Grandpa gave them a serious look. "No. Puns. Allowed."

"Huh?" Leo had not expected this.

"What's a pun?" asked Lizzie.

"It's kind of a joke," Leo told her. "Like remember how the Bumblers said 'buzz-iness'? It's actually 'business,' but they were talking about bees, so they said *buzz*-iness. Get it?"

Lizzie nodded. "So like a not-very-funny joke."

"Exactly," said Grandpa. "Don't make them." He started the engine again, then stepped on the gas. The truck lurched forward, scattering gravel behind them.

"Adventure!" Lizzie whooped. The kitten yowled.

Leo clutched his seat belt as they peeled out onto the road. All he could hope was that the adventure would be painless and over very soon.

CHAPTER 9

The problem with Grandpa's ban on puns was that suddenly Leo couldn't stop thinking of them. They piled up like questions in his head, practically begging to be let out.

This hive heist was un-bee-lievable!

Lizzie bringing along a kitten could be cat-astrophic.

If they didn't find the hives tonight, they'd need a Plan Bee.

Leo had no idea what the consequences for punning would be, and he definitely didn't want to find out. He bit his lip to keep them inside.

Fortunately (or rather, *un*fortunately), he soon found a good distraction: Grandpa's driving. Though the roads on Heron Island were narrow and twisty, Grandpa took them at alarming speeds, sometimes with one wheel teetering off the edge.

"Is there, um, a speed limit on the island?" Leo tried to sound calm as he tightened his seat belt.

"Of course not!" Grandpa scoffed. "At least, I don't think so," he added, as if he'd never thought about it before. "I've never seen a speed limit sign, and I've lived here for almost fifty years."

Leo found it hard to believe that Heron Island had no speed limit at all, but he could understand how someone might miss a sign, since the entire island appeared to be overgrown with vegetation. Moss blanketed the roof of nearly every house they passed. Ivy twisted up tree trunks and down fenceposts. Giant ferns choked the ditches on either side of the road.

It reminded him of a game called *Green Thumb,* which he and Santos had played last year. *Green Thumb* involved battling a deadly, carnivorous plant that preyed on unsuspecting humans as it spread through New York City. It had given Leo nightmares for weeks.

"So where are we going?" Lizzie asked as Grandpa sped into a hairpin turn. Leo grabbed the door handle and held on tight.

"To Béatriz's house," said Grandpa.

"Oh good, I like her." Lizzie held the kitten up to the window so she could watch the trees whiz by. "I bet she'll help us."

Grandpa shook his head. "We're going to inspect her property. I think she could be the thief."

"The *thief*?" Lizzie repeated.

"*Béatriz*?" said Leo.

"She knows the bees better than anyone, doesn't she? And whoever stole them had to know a lot about bees."

Leo frowned. He didn't know Béatriz well, but she didn't seem like someone who'd steal seven hundred thousand bees in the dead of night. "What about the other Bumblers then?" he asked. "Why do you suspect Béatriz, but not the rest of them?"

"Oh, I suspect them all," Grandpa replied. "This is just a place to start."

Leo wished he hadn't asked.

They zoomed up a hill and sped down the other side. Lizzie threw her hands in the air as if she were riding a roller coaster. Grandpa chuckled and sped on.

Was Grandpa an Adventurer too? Leo wondered as they swerved to avoid a squirrel scampering across the road. It certainly seemed like it, although, according to Fatefinder.com, Adventurers liked meeting new people, and that didn't seem true for Grandpa. But he clearly took risks without thinking critically.

Leo shook his head. Investigating a crime with two Adventurers felt like a recipe for disaster—they were bound to wind up in trouble. What they really needed was someone with a cool head who wouldn't go accusing an innocent person of theft. Someone who could gather clues and piece them together.

What they needed, he realized, was a Peregrine Peabody.

Peregrine Peabody, Private Eye had been Leo and Santos's favorite game back in fourth grade. In it, they'd played the role of a brilliant detective called on to solve all kinds of mysteries. They'd had to interview suspects, collect and analyze clues and come up with a solution to every crime. Leo had loved *Peregrine Peabody: Private Eye* (as well as its sequel, *Peregrine Peabody, Private Eye 2: Skeletons in the Closet*). And what's more, he was good at it. Even Santos, who excelled at all games, admitted that Leo was the superior detective.

Of course, detective definitely wasn't a career option in his Fatefinder.com profile. And yet—

Lizzie poked him in the ribs. "What should we name her?"

"Ow! What?"

She nodded at the kitten, who was mauling her sleeve with her tiny, razor-sharp teeth. "She needs a name that really suits her."

He sighed. "I don't think you should name—"

"We're naming her," said Lizzie. "Come on, you're good at this."

"Fine. How about Trouble?"

"That's cute," she said thoughtfully. "But not quite right."

"Chaos? Havoc? Mayhem?"

"Mayhem! Ooh, I like that! We can call her May for short. What do you think?" Lizzie asked the kitten. "Do you like your new name?"

Mayhem let go of Lizzie's arm and launched herself at a fly on the window, catching it between her paws. She played with it for a few moments before swallowing it whole.

"What a smart girl!" Lizzie cooed.

Leo felt sick. "Grandpa, are we almost there?"

"Getting close," he replied as they sailed past two teenagers standing on the edge of the road, holding their thumbs out. Grandpa raised a hand at them but didn't slow down.

"What are they doing?" asked Lizzie.

"Hitchhiking," said Grandpa. "That's how some islanders get around. People with extra space in their cars help people who need a lift."

"We had space." Lizzie pointed behind them at the truck bed.

"There aren't any seat belts back there," Leo observed.

"And more importantly, we're on a mission," said Grandpa. "There's no time for detours." He stepped on the gas and sped on.

Leo didn't think that was more important than a lack of seat belts, but he let it go. "Also, hitchhiking is dangerous," he added quietly, because knowing Lizzie, she'd be wandering the island with her thumb out the very next day. "Dad would lose his mind if you did it."

Grandpa turned off the narrow, twisty road onto a narrower, twistier one that wasn't even paved. They crunched along the gravel until they reached a rust-colored house with a bright blue door and window boxes over-flowing with flowers.

"Is this Béatriz's house?" Lizzie peered out the window. "It's so pretty."

Leo agreed. It definitely didn't look like the home of a bee thief, not that he'd ever seen one. "Grandpa, are you sure about this?" he asked. "Does Béatriz even have a motive for stealing the bees? A motive is like a reason for committing a crime," he added, in case Grandpa didn't know.

Grandpa ignored him and opened his door. "You two stay here while I go investigate."

"Wait, what are you going to—" Leo began, but Grandpa had already hopped out of the truck. He vaulted the ditch and took off running—not to Béatriz's front door, but straight into her backyard.

"Oh no," Leo moaned.

"I think Mayhem has to pee," said Lizzie.

"Of course she does." He unclipped his seat belt. "But how will you keep her with you?"

"I'm glad you asked!" She opened her backpack and pulled out a purple nylon rope. "Ta-da!"

Leo did a double take. "Is that a leash? You brought a *leash*?"

"And a matching collar!" Lizzie beamed. "I bought it at the pet store a few months ago. Pandora Ali always has a spare collar and leash in her purse, you know. She says you never know when you're going to meet a cat in need.

I wanted to buy them off her website, but I would have had to ask Mom or Dad for their credit card and, well, you know how that would have gone."

Leo could imagine. He watched as she carefully buckled the collar around Mayhem's neck, then clipped on the leash. The kitten shook her head, clawed the collar with her hind foot, then looked at Lizzie as if to say, "Now what"?

"She's going to be the perfect adventure cat," Lizzie said as they climbed out of the truck. "I'll train her to ride in my backpack with her head sticking out the top. Or maybe Mom and Dad will buy me a real cat backpack for my birthday! You know, the kind with the windows and air vents? Pandora Ali sells those on her website too."

While Mayhem did her business in the ditch and Lizzie jabbered on about cat backpacks, Leo watched Grandpa dart across Béatriz's backyard, headed for her vegetable patch. What would she do if she caught him? he wondered, hoping they wouldn't have to find out.

"Look, Leo!" Lizzie squealed. "Mayhem caught a mouse!"

"Gross." Leo turned away so he didn't have to watch, only to find himself suddenly face to face with a girl he'd never seen before. "Whoa!" he cried, stumbling backward into the ditch.

"Hello," the girl said calmly. She had curly black hair and dark eyes behind glasses with bright blue frames. She appeared to be around Leo's age.

"Um . . . hi?" He righted himself, wondering how long she'd been standing there.

"Oh, hi!" Lizzie said, as if welcoming an old friend and not a stranger who'd appeared out of nowhere. "Who are you?"

"Who are *you*?" the girl returned. She didn't seem upset—just curious.

"We're . . . uh . . ." Leo glanced at Grandpa just as he ducked into the vegetable patch.

"You're with Sam," she said matter-of-factly. "It's okay, we know he's out there. We heard you drive up while we were eating dinner. Sam's truck isn't exactly quiet, you know," she added. "I think he might need a new muffler."

"Oh." Leo cringed.

"I'm Lizzie," said Lizzie. "This is my brother, Leo, and this is our kitten, Mayhem. We call her May for short."

On cue, the kitten looked up from her kill. A long, skinny tail dangled from her mouth.

"Oh ew," Leo whispered.

The girl didn't seem fazed. "That's a good name," she said. "I'm Sofia. Sofi for short."

"That's a good name too." Lizzie smiled at her. Sofi smiled back.

Leo bristled. Another annoying thing about Lizzie was her ability to make friends with pretty well anyone.

"Sam doesn't think the bees are here, does he?" asked Sofi.

"Uh-huh," Lizzie said before Leo could stop her. "He doesn't trust anyone."

Leo gave her an exasperated look, then turned back to Sofi. "But *we* know the bees aren't here. At least, we assume they aren't. We met Béatriz . . . is she your mom?"

Sofi nodded.

"She made us lasagna," said Lizzie.

"I know," said Sofi. "We were going to bring it to you yesterday, but Mom got called in to do an emergency surgery at the hospital on Porpoise Island, so she got Jacques to deliver it. Did you meet Sawyer?"

"The kid?" Leo recalled the boy who'd dropped off the lasagna.

She nodded. "He's Jacques's nephew. He helps with deliveries and odd jobs and everything else Jacques does. He doesn't get paid, though. Except in wood."

"Wood?" Leo repeated.

"Sawyer's a woodworker," she explained. "Really talented too."

"Oh." Leo wasn't sure what else to say. He'd never known a kid woodworker.

"Anyway, back to the bees," Sofi went on. "Everyone is talking about their disappearance, you know. I'd say it's the biggest news on Heron Island since Mr. Lee slipped on the ferry deck, smacked his head and got knocked unconscious."

"Yikes!" said Lizzie.

"Yeah," said Sofi. "Fortunately, Mom was on board

that day and helped revive him. That story made the front page of the *Heron Herald*."

"Is that a newspaper?" Leo asked. She nodded.

Lizzie gasped. "Will Grandma's bees be in the newspaper? Will *we* be in the newspaper?"

"Maybe," said Sofi. "It's a really big deal. The person who stole them must have been a professional. I'm a beekeeper, and I wouldn't know how to steal that many bees."

"You're a beekeeper?" said Lizzie. "But you're so young!"

Sofi shrugged. "Anyone can be a beekeeper. I have five hives of my own, and I help Mom with hers. One day I'll probably take over the whole business."

"You mean *buzz*-iness?" Lizzie grinned.

"Lizzie," Leo warned her.

Sofi groaned at the pun, then paused, looking pensive. "We miss your Grandma a lot. She used to come over every spring to help us split our hives or build new boxes. She'd bring lemonade and caramel popcorn, and when the work was done, we'd have a party in the garden. Evelyn made the best caramel popcorn in the world. But of course you know that," she added. "Hey, do you have her recipe?"

Leo shook his head. In fact, he'd never tasted or even heard of Grandma's caramel popcorn, which was a huge disappointment because it was one of his favorite foods. He felt a stab of jealousy toward Sofi, who'd known his own grandma better than he had.

"There's Béatriz." Lizzie pointed. They watched Sofi's mom leave the house and walk toward Grandpa, who was peeking into her shed.

Leo cringed again. "So, um, will you be a beekeeper when you grow up?" he asked Sofi, hoping to distract from Grandpa's behavior.

"Well, I'm going to be a doctor like my mom," she said. "But I'll keep bees too—I want to train ours to detect cancer."

"Bees can detect *cancer*?" Leo had never heard of this.

She nodded. "Bombs too."

"*Bombs*?"

"Oh yeah, it's bananas! Scientists have trained bees to stick out their proboscises—"

"Their what?" Lizzie wrinkled her nose.

"The proboscis is like the bee's tongue—it's how they suck up nectar," Leo told her, pleased at the opportunity to show off his own bee knowledge. He didn't mention his virtual apiary, though—not to a real-life beekeeper.

"Right," said Sofi. "So these scientists trained their bees to stick out their proboscises when they came near explosives. That way they could tell where the bombs were just by looking at the bees. Bananas, right?"

"Bananas," Leo agreed.

"I love bees," Sofi said dreamily. "Did you know that they can recognize human faces?"

"Wow!" said Lizzie. "I love bees too."

Leo frowned at her. "You do *not*."

"I *do*," she insisted. "I just love cats more."

"Anyway," Sofi cut in, "where do you think you'll go next? Since clearly the bees aren't here."

Leo had no idea. He'd been hoping they could go straight home to bed.

She tapped her chin thoughtfully. "One of the Bumblers sent my mom an article about a big hive heist in the States. Apparently, millions of bees were stolen in Montana and trucked to California, where almond growers need bees to pollinate their trees. You should find the article online. Maybe it'll help your investigation."

It was a good idea, Leo agreed. "Except Grandpa doesn't have the internet."

"No internet?" Sofi gasped. "Not at *all*?"

He shook his head. "Do most people on Heron Island have internet?"

"Of course!" She looked offended. "We're not totally backward."

"Oh, I didn't mean—"

"Do you have a phone?" She pulled hers out of her pocket.

"Um, yeah."

"Give it here. I'll connect you to our Wi-Fi network. It's superfast."

An internet connection! Leo fumbled for his phone, unlocked it and handed it over.

"You search for that article and download it," Sofi instructed when she gave the phone back. "And I'll make you a map on my phone. It'll show you all the most important spots on Heron Island. You can download that too so you can access it when you don't have a connection." Her thumbs moved swiftly across her screen.

"Wow! Thanks!" Leo couldn't believe she was being so helpful, especially with Grandpa snooping through her backyard. Minutes later, his phone buzzed, and he opened the file she'd sent.

"Let me see." Lizzie leaned into him. "Does that say ice cream?"

"The best on the island," said Sofi. "Actually, it's the only ice cream on the island, but still really good. I also marked the café—Mr. Lee makes delicious cinnamon buns. He's the one who got knocked unconscious on the ferry. But he's fine now."

"Wait." Leo zoomed in on the map. "Does this say . . . *feral goats*?"

She nodded. "I thought you should know. Feral means wild."

"There are *wild goats* on Heron Island?"

"Cool!" shouted Lizzie. "I'm really good at taming wild animals," she told Sofi.

"I wouldn't try that," Sofi advised. "They can be grumpy. Just don't bother them and they won't bother you. Hey, that reminds me: do either of you play *Applewood Acres*?"

"What?" Leo nearly dropped his phone. "YES!"

"I just got *Applewood Acres 4: Shenanigoats*. Have you heard of it?"

Had he heard of it! Leo felt like leaping for joy. He was about to tell her that he'd been waiting for months to play *Shenanigoats,* that it was rumored to be the best sequel yet, even better than *Applewood Acres 2: Hog Wild,* which was really—

She gasped. "He's coming. I should go."

Leo turned to see Grandpa stomping toward them. When he turned back to Sofi, she was already jogging away.

"Bye, Leo, bye, Lizzie!" she called. "Bye, Mayhem!"

"Bye, Sofi!" Lizzie shouted. "I like her," she said to Leo.

He nodded and waved goodbye, wondering if Grandpa might drive him back to Sofi's one day so they could play *Applewood Acres 4: Shenanigoats.*

"Everyone back in the truck!" Grandpa commanded. "We're getting out of here!"

Leo sighed. There was no way. He pocketed his phone and climbed back into the truck.

CHAPTER 10

"You didn't find anything, did you, Grandpa?" Lizzie asked as they drove away from Béatriz's house.

Grandpa grumble-huffed in reply.

"So where to now?"

"Maybe home?" Leo suggested quickly. The sun was close to setting, and the sky was streaked with violet and pink. Soon it would be dark. Very, very dark.

"We'll just make one more stop," said Grandpa. "You're not tired, are you?"

Leo nodded vigorously, although he actually wasn't. He threw in a yawn for effect.

"Not me!" Lizzie proclaimed. "I'm a night owl. Mayhem is too. Grandpa, did you know that cats aren't actually nocturnal? They're crepuscular—that means they're active at dawn and dusk. I did a science fair project on cat behavior, you know."

"I see," said Grandpa. "Well, I'm a night owl too."

Leo slumped in his seat, outnumbered again. "Fine. Where are we going now?"

"To Bruno's," Grandpa replied, picking up speed.

"Bruno...the Bumbler?" Leo recalled the man perched on the kitchen counter, swinging his very long legs.

"Bruno the Bumbler." Grandpa hung a sharp right—without signaling, Leo noted. "He lives at the north end of the island. It's about a half-hour drive."

"We'll get comfortable." Lizzie kicked off her sneakers and put her feet up on the dashboard. Tucked inside her hoodie, Mayhem began to purr.

Leo was not about to get comfortable. Instead, he took out his phone and opened Sofi's map so he could track their progress. He still couldn't believe that in the middle of nowhere on Heron Island, he'd met someone who played *Applewood Acres.* He wondered if Sofi had ever played *Green Thumb* or *Peregrine Peabody: Private Eye.*

Which reminded him: he had detective work to do.

He cleared his throat and turned to Grandpa. "Why do you think Bruno stole the bees? Does he have a motive?"

Grandpa didn't answer.

"A motive is a reason for committing—"

"I know what it is!" Grandpa snapped.

"Then what's his motive?" Now Leo was growing impatient too.

Grandpa paused for a moment, then began to explain. "Every fall, Bruno organizes the annual Heron Island

Honey Festival. It's a big to-do, with food and music and far too many people, in my opinion. But the most important part of the festival is the honey-tasting competition. Beekeepers from all the islands bring samples of their honey, and a sommelier comes from Vancouver to judge and hand out prizes."

"What's a sommelier?" asked Leo.

"Someone who tastes things for a living," Grandpa replied.

"That's a *job*?" Leo had never heard of this.

"I'd be good at that!" Lizzie piped up. "Dad says I have an adventurous palate."

Leo rolled his eyes. "So the sweetest honey wins the competition?"

"It's more complicated than that," said Grandpa. "The judge looks at the color, clarity and water content of the honey, as well as the taste. Did you know that some honeys taste like the blossoms the bees drink nectar from?"

"Really?" Leo had never considered that honey tasted like anything but, well, honey.

"Really," said Grandpa. "Anyway, Evelyn's bees made the most delicious honey around. For the last three years, she took home the top prize: Honey of the Year."

"Wow."

He nodded. "Last year, Evelyn dropped off her entries at Bruno's the night before the contest, like she always did.

But the next day, when the judging began, they were nowhere to be found, and Bruno swore he hadn't seen them. Now, I don't know what happened, but I know darn well Evelyn dropped off that honey."

"Why would Bruno sabotage the honey competition?" Leo asked. "Did he end up winning Honey of the Year?"

"Nope," Grandpa said. "Marguerite did."

"The president of the Bumblers?"

"That's right."

Leo frowned. "So why aren't we investigating her?"

"We are," Grandpa said, making a sharp left turn. "They're married."

"Oh!" He sat up straight. "So you think they were working together? Like, in cahoots?" "In cahoots" was one of Peregrine Peabody's favorite phrases.

"Possibly," said Grandpa.

Leo pondered this as they made their way to the north end of the island. The disappearance of Grandma's honey did sound suspicious. But even if Bruno and Marguerite had sabotaged the honey competition, would they go so far as to steal Grandma's bees? And then sit in Grandpa's kitchen and pretend they hadn't?

"I'll just take a quick look around their farm," said Grandpa. "By the time we get there it'll be nice and dark."

Leo pictured him stumbling around in the pitch-darkness. "Do you have a flashlight?"

He shook his head. "I have pretty good night vision."

"Like a cat," Lizzie put in. "Did you know that cats—"

"We know," Leo interrupted, then turned back to Grandpa. "But how will you know if you find Grandma's hives? Do they look different from other people's hives?"

Grandpa opened his mouth to reply, then shut it. After a moment's pause, he said, "I'll just know."

"Maybe the bees will recognize you!" Lizzie chirped. "They can recognize human faces, you know."

Leo took a deep breath and turned back to his map.

"What have you got there?" asked Grandpa.

"A map of the island," he replied. He didn't mention where he'd gotten it.

"Look for Salt Bay Road. That's where we're headed."

Leo found it at the very northern tip of the island, right beside Sofi's note about the feral goats.

"Grandpa, are there, um, wild goats around there?" he asked, trying to sound casual.

"There sure are," Grandpa replied. "And they can be mean. Did your mom tell you about them?"

This was a good question. Why *hadn't* Mom warned him about the dangerous wildlife on the island? He shook his head, then glanced at Lizzie. Her eyes were closed, her chin resting on Mayhem's head. "You know it's past Lizzie's bedtime, right?"

"No, it's not!" She sat bolt upright and drove her elbow into his ribs.

"Ow! Lizzie!"

"I'm not tired, Grandpa," she assured him.

Grandpa switched on the truck's headlights. "We won't be long. And you can sleep in here if you want. There should be a blanket around somewhere."

Leo couldn't imagine a worse place to sleep. Even Lizzie grimaced.

"It'll be like camping," said Grandpa. "You've been camping, haven't you?"

Leo recalled the one time they'd gone, when he was eight years old and Lizzie was six. Looking back, he couldn't imagine why Mom and Dad had wanted to go— neither of them liked camping to begin with, and by the end of the trip they both despised it. Their tent had leaked. They'd forgotten their pasta at home and ended up eating plain tomato sauce for dinner. Then Lizzie had found a tick embedded in her shoulder and Dad had freaked out about Lyme disease and insisted they find a doctor straight away. On the way out of the campground, he'd pulled the car over and thrown the entire leaky tent in the trash bin.

"Once," Leo told Grandpa. "We went once."

"Once!" Grandpa scoffed. "That's not enough. You two should be sleeping outside under the stars, cooking your food over a fire. It's a formative experience." He thumped the steering wheel with the heel of his hand.

"What's a formative experience?" asked Lizzie.

"It's . . ." He paused. "It's something that makes you the person you're supposed to be."

Leo wondered if a formative experience could make him something other than an Auditor. Could sleeping outside under the stars and cooking over a campfire do that? Would it be worth it to try? He considered this as they continued northward into the deepening darkness.

"Do you like camping, Grandpa?" Lizzie asked, sounding sleepy.

"Like it!" he exclaimed. "I love it! I spent most of my twenties camping, back when I worked for a logging company in the mountains. I often slept right on the ground, without a tent. Sometimes without a sleeping bag, if it wasn't too cold."

Leo shivered. He definitely wasn't up for that kind of formative experience.

About twenty minutes later, they emerged from the forest into a swath of farmland. The moon was rising to the east above a small, white house.

"Are we there?" asked Leo.

"We're here." Grandpa pulled off the road and parked in front of a rusty, old car that looked like it hadn't moved in years.

Leo squinted at the house, which was dark except for a light in one window on the second floor. He hoped Bruno and Marguerite were already asleep. And that they didn't have a dog that would alert them to intruders. Especially not a big dog with sharp teeth. Leo chewed his lip as Grandpa opened his door and hopped out.

"I won't be long," Grandpa whispered. Then he hurried off toward the house, once again leaving Leo and Lizzie alone in the truck. Lizzie put her head on Leo's shoulder; within moments she was snoring.

Could all Adventurers fall asleep anywhere, anytime? Leo wondered. Maybe that explained how Grandpa could camp without a tent, or even a sleeping bag.

To pass the time and distract himself from the darkening night, he pulled out his phone and opened the article he'd downloaded at Sofi's—the story of the beekeeper whose hives went missing in Montana and showed up weeks later in California. The article explained that the almond industry required billions of bees for pollination, so every spring, beekeepers from across the U.S. sent millions of hives to California, where the almond growers paid to borrow them. Some brazen thieves had begun to take advantage of this, stealing unsuspecting beekeepers' hives and renting them to the almond growers, who had no idea they were stolen.

Leo was just debating whether he ought to tell Grandpa what he'd learned or keep quiet about it in case Grandpa decided to drag them to California, when he heard someone shout.

A dog began to bark—a big one, by the sound of it. Leo sat up straight. Lizzie's head rolled off his shoulder.

Someone shouted again. "Hey! You!"

"Oh no." Leo squinted out the window, but it was too dark to see anything. Moments later, he heard footsteps approaching. Then the truck door swung open, and Grandpa leaped inside.

"What happened?" Leo cried.

Grandpa jammed his key into the ignition. "We're leaving!" he barked, turning the key and stepping on the gas pedal.

But instead of moving forward, the truck rolled *backward*—right into the car parked behind them.

CRUNCH.

Leo gasped. Grandpa swore.

That woke Lizzie up. "What's going on?"

"We hit a car!" Leo twisted in his seat, trying to assess the damage.

"No, we didn't!" Grandpa put the truck in drive and stepped on the gas again.

"Wait, what are you doing?" Leo spun to look at him. "Grandpa, you can't leave!" He'd never been in an accident before, and he'd only driven a car in a game called *Hotwire* (which was banned from his collection when Dad declared that ten-year-olds shouldn't be stealing cars, even virtual ones). But even he knew that when a driver hit another vehicle, they couldn't just up and leave. That was a crime.

"Oh, we're leaving!" Grandpa declared, picking up speed.

Leo clutched the door handle and tried to think straight. "I think . . . you're supposed to leave a note?"

Grandpa snorted. "Are you crazy?"

96

Lizzie found Leo's hand and squeezed it. He knew that meant she was scared.

"Grandpa!" he said firmly. "We can't just leave. When you hit a parked car, you *have to leave a note!*"

Even as he said it, he knew it was ridiculous. The car probably hadn't moved in years, and Bruno and Marguerite might well know exactly who'd hit it. But driving away was wrong. Just like sneaking onto other people's property was wrong. In fact, everything about this stupid mission was wrong!

"We are not leaving a note!" Grandpa declared, gripping the steering wheel.

"Well, WE SHOULD!" Leo shouted back.

The kitten let out a cry. She wiggled out of Lizzie's hoodie and jumped down onto the floor. "Mayhem!" Lizzie cried. "Catch her, Leo!" She unbuckled her seat belt and slid off the seat.

"Lizzie, don't!"

"SIT DOWN!" Grandpa roared.

Lizzie froze, then burst into tears.

"Oh great," Leo spat. "Way to go, Grandpa." He scooped the kitten up off the floor and handed her back to Lizzie, then buckled her back in.

Grandpa drew a long, grumbling breath. "Listen. I need you to be quiet and let me drive. We are *not* leaving a note. We are *going home.*"

"It's okay," Leo whispered to Lizzie as her sobs turned to sniffles and Mayhem slunk back into her hoodie.

Minutes later, the kitten was purring and Lizzie's head was lolling once more.

Leo, on the other hand, wasn't sure he'd ever sleep again. In one night, Grandpa had been caught trespassing on two properties, hit a car *and* fled the scene of the crime. *Three* crimes in *one* night! Without any regard for Leo and Lizzie's feelings, or more importantly their criminal records.

"That really stings," Leo muttered. It was absolutely a pun, but he didn't care. If Grandpa didn't have to follow rules, then neither would he.

CHAPTER 11

When Leo opened his eyes the next morning, he found himself looking at a foggy windshield. He closed his eyes, certain he was dreaming, but when he opened them again, the scene hadn't changed: he was still in Grandpa's truck. Lizzie snored beside him, her head on his shoulder. Beside her, Grandpa slept with his hat pulled down over his face.

Leo wiped the windshield with his sleeve and peered out. They were parked outside Grandpa's house.

"What the heck?" he whispered. Why weren't they inside?

He pulled out his phone, which told him it was seven o'clock. Then he tried to remember how the previous night had ended, after Grandpa had sneaked onto Bruno and Marguerite's property, backed into their car, driven away without leaving a note *and* made Lizzie cry. He could recall driving home in the dark, but he couldn't remember arriving. He and Lizzie must have fallen asleep, and Grandpa let them stay that way.

It was a suitable end to a terrible night.

He sighed, then screamed as something stabbed him in the leg.

Grandpa sat bolt upright. "What is it? What's wrong?"

"Mayhem!" Leo grabbed the kitten, who'd just dug her claws into his thigh.

"Mayhem?" Lizzie mumbled.

"Mayhem." He dropped her into Lizzie's lap.

She rubbed her eyes. "Where are we?"

"And *why* are we here?" Leo rubbed his thigh where Mayhem had scratched him.

Grandpa yawned. "You were both asleep by the time we got back last night. I didn't want to move you."

"We slept in a truck?" Lizzie gasped. "That's so cool!"

Leo did not agree. Sleeping in Grandpa's cold and smelly old truck was basically camping!

Had that been Grandpa's plan? he wondered. To make his indoorsy grandkids sleep outside? To give them a "formative experience"?

He glowered. That would be *so* like Grandpa.

"Can we get breakfast?" Lizzie asked. "I'm starving. I'd even eat the old shredded wheat."

"Yup," said Grandpa. "Or we could go to the café for breakfast. You like cinnamon buns?"

"I LOVE cinnamon buns!" she cried.

"Good." He started the truck. "We'll get the best on the island."

Leo recalled Sofi saying that the best cinnamon buns were made by Mr. Lee, who'd been knocked unconscious on the ferry but was apparently fine now. His stomach rumbled—he loved cinnamon buns too, especially when they were topped with cream cheese icing. But he didn't say so to Grandpa. He didn't say anything at all.

"The cafe has Wi-Fi," Grandpa added as he backed the truck down the driveway. "If you want the internet, Leo."

If he wanted the internet?! *Of course* he wanted the internet! Still, he said nothing. If Grandpa thought cinnamon buns and Wi-Fi would make him forget what had happened, he could think again. Because Leo was *done.* Done searching for missing bees. Done keeping Lizzie out of trouble. Done with islands ruled by untamed vegetation and angry wild goats.

And most of all, he was done—completely DONE— with Grandpa.

As soon as they reached the café, he decided, he would slip away, call Mom and Dad and tell them everything. Everything! And he'd demand—yes, DEMAND—they return to Heron Island right away. He didn't care if they called him the family Auditor. He just couldn't do it anymore.

Grandpa drove more slowly that morning, winding his way to the south end of the island toward the ferry termi- nal and the town, if you could call it a town. According to

Sofi's map, it had a grocery store, a hardware store, a pub, a health clinic and their destination: the Driftwood Café.

Leo wasn't sure what to expect from the café, but he hoped it would be something like Cool Beans, the coffee shop across the street from their condo. Cool Beans had air conditioning and a neat line of tables where people would sit for hours, sipping espressos and typing on their laptops. It was Dad's favorite spot to research new career paths.

"Here we are," Grandpa said as he pulled off the road into a parking lot.

"*This* is the café?" Lizzie laughed.

Leo stared in disbelief. The Driftwood Café looked absolutely nothing like Cool Beans. In fact, it didn't even look like a café! It was an old house painted eggplant-purple with lime-green trim. On the front porch was a big swing, and the yard was overgrown with wildflowers and surrounded by a fence made of driftwood.

"This is the café," Grandpa confirmed. He pulled some crumpled bills out of his wallet and handed them to Leo. "Get three cinnamon buns. And a large coffee for me."

"*I'm* getting them?" said Leo. "You're not coming in?"

Grandpa shook his head. "Nah."

"Why not?" Leo asked. Then it occurred to him. "Are you afraid of getting arrested?"

"Arrested!" Grandpa snorted. "What for?"

"For hitting Bruno and Marguerite's car and fleeing the scene of the crime," Leo reminded him.

"Of course not!"

"Then why won't you come in?" he persisted.

Grandpa gave him an incredulous look. "Do you *ever* stop asking questions?"

"No," Leo returned evenly.

Grandpa let out a grumble-huff. "Look, do you want breakfast or not?"

"Yes, he does," Lizzie cut in. "And so does Mayhem. Come on, Leo." She snapped the kitten's leash onto her collar. "I'll help her hunt while you get the cinnamon buns."

"Fine," Leo grumbled. He opened the door and slid out.

While Lizzie led Mayhem into the wildflowers, Leo walked up the steps of the house and peered through the open front door. Whoever had painted the outside of the house must have had leftover paint, since all the interior walls were eggplant purple too. A lime-green couch sat in the middle of the room, and mismatched tables and chairs were arranged haphazardly around it. It looked more like a very strange living room than a café, but it did smell delicious: like butter and sugar and cinnamon.

Leo spotted a counter piled high with cinnamon buns topped with cream cheese, just the way he liked them. He hurried across the room toward it, then stopped when someone shouted, "Leo!"

He turned to see Jin the Bumbler ambling toward him, wearing paint-splattered overalls. "Fancy seeing you here!"

"Oh! Hi." Leo was surprised to see him too. "Um, are you Mr. Lee?"

"I sure am." Jin grinned. "Owner of the Driftwood Café and baker of the best cinnamon buns on Heron Island. I assume that's what you came for?"

"But . . . I thought you were a beekeeper," said Leo.

"I do that too," said Jin. "I also dabble in painting, but that's more of a hobby."

Leo recalled Grandpa saying that some people on Heron Island had more than one job. Clearly Jin was one of them.

"Willa, look who dropped in!" Jin called to a woman at a table in the corner, whom Leo hadn't noticed. It took him a moment to recognize Willa the Bumbler, who no longer had a shower cap over her silver curls. She smiled and raised her teacup.

Leo waved back. Was this why Grandpa had refused to come inside? he wondered. Had he known there would be Bumblers?

"So what can I get for you?" asked Jin.

"Three cinnamon buns and a coffee to go, please," Leo told him.

"You got it. Cream and sugar for the coffee?"

Leo frowned. "I'm not sure. It's for my grandpa."

"Hmm." Jin glanced over at Willa. "I bet he takes his coffee black."

She nodded, looking nervously at the door, as if expecting Grandpa to storm in.

It was as good a guess as any, so Leo agreed and paid for the order. While Jin was preparing it, he pulled out his phone, ready to call Mom and Dad and tell them what had happened. But when he tried to switch the phone on, he realized the battery was dead.

"Nooo," he groaned. His charger, of course, was back at Grandpa's.

"Three cinnamon buns and a coffee to go!" Jin plopped them on the counter. "Now, you have to let me know what you think."

Leo looked up from his phone. "About the cinnamon buns?"

Jin shook his head, then pointed to Leo's left. On the wall beside the cash register, someone had painted a woman's face, about five times larger than life. She had straight, gray hair and a round face, but what Leo noticed most was her big, toothy smile.

It was the same smile she'd worn all day at the aquarium downtown.

"It's Grandma!" he exclaimed.

What's more, she was surrounded by bees! They swarmed around her head like little fireflies on the purple wall.

Jin looked pleased. "It's a memorial mural. Marguerite came up with the idea, and I painted it. I'm not quite finished—I really want her eyes to sparkle. And I have to add the notes, of course. Hey, do you want to help me with that? We could do it right now."

"Notes?" Leo tore his eyes away from Grandma and glanced at the door. What would Grandpa say if he found him working on the memorial wall with Jin? Did he even know about it?

"You'll love this, Leo." Jin produced a stack of colorful sticky notes from the pocket of his overalls and explained that he'd asked his customers to write down their favorite memories of Evelyn. "Stick them to the wall, wherever you want," he said, handing Leo the notes. "I might rearrange them later."

Leo read the note on the top of the pile:

Evelyn volunteered at the health clinic every Tuesday for 20 years! We couldn't have done our work without her.

The next one said:

Evelyn shared her beekeeping knowledge with anyone who needed it. She was so generous with her time!

He read on. Evelyn organized the musical theater troupe. She helped survey local seabird populations. She taught all the kids on the island how to catch and hold hermit crabs without hurting them.

"Wow," Leo whispered, sifting through the notes. Grandpa wasn't kidding when he said Grandma had done everything.

Then he came upon a note that made him freeze.

I'll never forget this bee-autiful soul's undying love of puns!

"Puns?" Leo read it again just to be sure. He flipped to the next note.

You just couldn't help POLLEN in love with Evelyn!

"*Puns?*" he repeated.

"Oh, Evelyn loved puns." Jin chuckled. "When she started punning, there was no stopping her."

"Is *that* why Grandpa hates them so much?" Leo wondered.

Jin's smile faded, and he sighed. "Grief is complicated, Leo."

Leo recalled Mom saying the same thing their first night at Grandpa's. He swallowed and handed the notes back. "I should go."

Jin passed him the cinnamon buns and coffee. "Come back anytime, okay?"

"Okay." Leo thanked him and hurried back outside.

Grandpa and Lizzie were sitting on the grass near the truck, and Mayhem was slinking through the wildflowers beside them, probably hunting her own breakfast. Leo joined them and handed out the cinnamon buns. He wanted to mention the mural—it felt wrong not to tell Lizzie about it. But he wasn't sure what Grandpa would say, so he kept quiet and mulled it over while he ate.

The cinnamon buns were delicious, as Sofi had promised. Did she know about Grandma's love of puns too? Leo wished he could ask her. She seemed like the kind of person you could mull things over with.

They sat in the grass and ate their cinnamon buns, and Leo thought about the Grandma that everyone on Heron Island had known, the one who volunteered at the health clinic and surveyed seabird populations and helped people split their beehives in the springtime. Then he thought about all the times Mom had passed him the phone when she was talking to Grandma and how awkward he'd felt answering her questions about school and swimming lessons. He'd always tried to end those conversations quickly and pass the phone back.

He couldn't remember ever asking Grandma about herself. And apparently there had been so much to know!

"Hey, Leo." Lizzie interrupted his musings. "If Mayhem took the Fatefinder test, what do you think she'd be?"

He shook his head. Mayhem's Fatefinder profile was truly the last thing he wanted to think about.

"I'm pretty sure she's an Adventurer." Lizzie scooped Mayhem up and started to dance among the wildflowers.

"I'm pretty sure you've had too much sugar," he muttered. Then he turned to Grandpa, who was sipping his coffee and staring into the distance. "Hey, Grandpa."

Grandpa hummed into his coffee cup.

As usual, Leo had so many questions—about the mural,

about Grandma and her love of puns. He had no idea which was most important.

And then it came to him. "Can we keep looking for the bees?"

Grandpa looked surprised. "You want to?"

"Yeah." He wanted to do it for Grandma, even though he'd never really known her. Or maybe *because* he'd never really known her.

"I figured you were done with investigating after last night." Grandpa took a swig of coffee.

"I was," said Leo. "But I think it's important."

Grandpa regarded him for a moment, then nodded. "Okay. We'll keep looking."

"But Grandpa," Leo added as another thought came to mind. "Can we, um, maybe not trespass on people's property anymore?"

Grandpa considered this, then nodded again. "All right."

"All right?" Leo hadn't expected him to be so reasonable.

"Sure."

"Well, okay then." Leo finished his cinnamon bun and wiped his sticky fingers on the grass. It was time to channel his inner Peregrine Peabody. "So what should we investigate next? Can you think of any other suspects? Maybe someone involved in that honey festival?"

Grandpa scratched his chin. "Well, there is one guy . . ."

Leo waited, hoping this suspect would have what Peregrine Peabody called "a plausible motive."

"A few years ago, he asked Evelyn to help him set up some hives. He knew nothing about bees, and of course she knew everything. She gave him a few lessons and invited him to join the Bumblers, but he wasn't interested."

"So what happened?" asked Leo. "Did he compete in the honey festival?"

"Oh no," said Grandpa. "He lost all his bees in an unseasonable cold snap, then gave up beekeeping."

For a moment Leo felt bad for the guy, remembering the demise of his own bees. Then he saw what Grandpa was getting at. "You think he stole Grandma's hives because his own bees died?"

Grandpa shrugged. "Maybe."

"That's a plausible motive," Leo said. "Who is this guy?"

Grandpa set his empty coffee cup on the ground and crushed it with his heel. "Jacques."

"Of All Trades?" Leo pictured the man sitting in his truck while his nephew delivered lasagna to Grandpa's door.

"That's the one." Grandpa stood up and stretched. "He lives on top of Heron Mountain. There's a road that goes up there, but only residents can use it. We'll have to hike."

"Wait, we're going to *hike*?" said Leo. "Up a *mountain*?" He had not expected this.

Grandpa scoffed. "They call it a mountain, but it's only a hill. It's just a little hike, with a great view at the top."

"Oh. Okay." Leo looked over at Lizzie, who was now turning cartwheels in the grass. A little hike would probably be good for her. "But no trespassing, right?" he said, just to be sure.

"No trespassing," said Grandpa. "Now let's get going."

CHAPTER 12

"Just a little hike," Leo muttered as he pushed aside a fern the size of his sister. "Just a little hike up a *giant mountain*."

"It wouldn't have been so bad if we'd stayed on the trail," Lizzie puffed behind him.

He grunted in agreement. It had started out fine: they'd left the truck where the public road ended at the base of Heron Mountain and followed a gravel trail into the forest. But after about ten minutes, Grandpa declared that he knew a shortcut and marched off into the trees, leaving Leo and Lizzie no choice but to follow. The "shortcut" climbed straight up the side of Heron Mountain, which, despite Grandpa's claim that it wasn't a real mountain, was steeper than any hill Leo had ever seen. After half an hour of scrambling over moss-covered boulders and trudging through ankle-deep mud, they were scraped and bruised and covered in dirt. And still nowhere near the top.

So much for Grandpa being reasonable. Leo grunted again, louder this time, so he might hear.

"Remember that time the elevator broke in our building?" Lizzie wheezed.

Leo nodded. For three days, they'd had to climb fourteen flights of stairs to get to their condo after school. It had made their lungs burn and their calves cramp up.

"This is worse," they agreed.

"Pick up the pace!" Grandpa called over his shoulder. "We're almost there!"

"Ow!"

Leo looked back and saw Lizzie on the ground, having tripped over a tree root the size of a boa constrictor. He helped her up and checked on Mayhem, who was sitting calmly in her backpack. Lizzie had left the top unzipped so Mayhem could poke her head out and take in the sights and smells of the forest. Leo couldn't say for certain, but it looked like Mayhem was actually enjoying herself.

"How much longer?" he shouted.

Grandpa turned around. "You're not tired already, are you?"

Leo and Lizzie looked at each other, then nodded.

"Only ten minutes or so." Grandpa hopped over a fallen log and continued on.

"What's he going to do when we get there?" Lizzie asked as Leo helped her over the log.

Leo wasn't sure. "Maybe he'll go talk to Jacques. Or maybe he'll just look over his fence. Either way, he's not going to trespass."

"You mean like what he did last night?" Lizzie asked.

Leo nodded. "He promised not to this time."

"Huh. So what's that about?" She pointed at a sign nailed to the tree that Grandpa had just passed. It read: PRIVATE PROPERTY. KEEP OUT!

"Grandpa!" Leo shouted.

"What *now*?"

"I think you're on . . ." He lowered his voice to a loud whisper. "Jacques's property!"

Grandpa waved him off. "Come on, we're almost there."

"Grandpa!" Leo couldn't believe it. "You're trespassing!"

Finally, Grandpa stopped. "I am not!"

Leo pointed up at the sign. "You said—"

"Oh, come on!" Grandpa threw his hands in the air, exasperated. "Haven't you ever heard of the right to roam?"

Leo and Lizzie shook their heads.

"Well." He took off his hat and wiped his forehead. "In some countries, like Norway and Scotland, you can roam anywhere you want, even if it's on someone else's land. You can even camp anywhere so long as you respect the environment. And that's the way it should be." He put his hat back on. "I'm just exercising my right to roam."

Leo was skeptical. "Is that the rule on Heron Island? Do we actually have the right to roam here?"

"That's not the point," Grandpa snapped. "On principle, we should be allowed to roam anywhere."

"So does that mean we can?" asked Lizzie.

"No," Leo said, just as Grandpa said, "Yes."

They glared at each other.

"Can't we just talk to Jacques?" asked Leo.

Grandpa raised an eyebrow. "You think he'll just come out and tell us he stole the bees?"

Leo flushed. "Well, we wouldn't ask him *directly*." But before he could tell Grandpa what he'd learned about interviewing suspects from Peregrine Peabody, Grandpa had started off again.

"You two stay here," he called back. "I'll take a quick look around and come straight back. Okay?"

It was definitely not okay. But there was no arguing with Grandpa, who had already tromped off, leaving them alone in the middle of the forest, on the side of a mountain.

"I think Mayhem needs a break." Lizzie lowered her backpack onto the forest floor and opened it so the kitten could hop out. Mayhem sniffed the air, then opened her mouth wide, showing off her sharp, little teeth.

"Oh, look!" Lizzie exclaimed. "She's sucking the smells into her vomeronasal organ! That's a group of cells on the roof of her mouth—it helps her understand what she's smelling. Isn't that cool?"

"Sure." Leo sank down onto a log, then on second thought hopped back up and did a quick scan for spiders and snakes. Seeing none, he flopped down again.

"Leo!"

"*What*?"

"She's scratching a piece of wood, see?"

He sighed. "So what?"

"Cats scratch to mark their territory," Lizzie explained. "But they also do it to stretch their muscles or show feelings like stress and excitement. I bet she's excited right now. What do you think?"

He shrugged, too tired and irritated to care.

Lizzie knelt in the dirt beside Mayhem. "It looks a bit like a scratch pad on Pandora Ali's website, but not as nice. Pandora's are turquoise and bright pink. And super expensive. Hey, Leo?"

"I don't care," he moaned.

"It says 'HIVE A.'"

"Huh?"

"Look." She picked up the wood and brought it over. On one side, close to the jagged edge where it had been broken, were the letters HIVE A. "Think it's part of a beehive?"

Leo sat up and examined the wood. Did beekeepers label their hives alphabetically? he wondered. He'd never labeled his hives in *Applewood Acres 3: What's the Buzz?* but maybe Heron Island beekeepers were different. "Let's ask Grandpa when he gets back."

They didn't have to wait long. About five minutes later, Grandpa tromped back through the forest, cursing under his breath.

"Did you find them?" asked Lizzie.

He shook his head. "I looked everywhere I could. Jacques's place is on a steep hill—there aren't many spots where the ground is level enough for beehives."

"Look what Mayhem found." Lizzie showed him the scratch pad. "It says 'HIVE A,' see?"

"Did Grandma label her hives alphabetically?" asked Leo. "Like, HIVE A, HIVE B, HIVE C . . ."

Grandpa studied their find. "I don't think so. She never mentioned anything about that."

"Oh." Leo was disappointed. It had seemed like a plausible clue.

"Too bad," Lizzie agreed. "But at least Mayhem gets a scratch pad." She slipped it into her backpack along with the kitten. "So what do we do now?"

Grandpa squinted up at the treetops. "Well, we're almost at the peak. Want to see the view?"

Leo and Lizzie exchanged a glance.

He sighed. "We can get back on the trail if you really want. It's not far."

"I want to see it," said Lizzie. "If it's *really* not that far."

"Would I lie?" said Grandpa. Before they could answer, he set off again.

Thankfully, this time he was true to his word. Within minutes they were back on the trail, hiking on gravel instead of moss and mud.

"So much better!" said Lizzie. Leo agreed.

They began to climb again, but it was easier now with no obstacles in the way. Soon the forest grew brighter and the gravel underfoot turned to smooth, bare rock. And then suddenly, they were there, at the top of Heron Mountain.

"Cool!" Lizzie shouted.

"See?" Grandpa sounded smug. "I told you."

Leo had always thought the view from their fourteenth-floor condo was spectacular. But it had nothing on the view from the top of Heron Mountain. The gray-blue Pacific Ocean seemed to stretch on forever, speckled with whitecaps and rippled with currents. Here and there, other islands rose out of the water like big, green sea creatures.

"Wow," he breathed, taking it all in. Then he noticed a few rooftops on the hillside below them. "Which house is Jacques's?"

Grandpa pointed to the one on the right. "He has a million-dollar view."

Leo tried to imagine what it would be like to look out on the ocean and the islands every day. It made him feel small and insignificant, but somehow also brave and capable. And maybe even a tiny bit adventurous?

"Which island is Porpoise Island?" asked Lizzie.

Grandpa pointed at a large island to the east. Its shoreline was dotted with colorful little houses.

"It's pretty," said Lizzie. "We should go there."

Leo expected Grandpa to scoff, but instead he nodded. "Actually, I've been thinking about that. How would you two feel about a little trip to Porpoise Island?"

"Really?" Lizzie gasped.

"I thought you hated Porpoise Island," Leo said, remembering Grandpa's reaction when Dad had suggested he accompany them to the resort.

"I don't hate all of it," said Grandpa. "Anyway, there are a lot of beekeepers there to investigate. And I have a friend there who might be able to help us."

Lizzie gasped again. "You have a *friend*?"

He sniffed. "Of course I have a friend. Mo is the most helpful person I know."

Leo frowned, still trying to wrap his head around this change in plans. "So we'd take the ferry?"

"Well, we're not going to swim," said Grandpa. "It's one-thirty now, and the boat leaves at three o'clock. We'd be there by four. What do you say? It would just be a quick visit."

"Sounds like an adventure! May and I are in," Lizzie declared.

Leo hesitated. "Just a quick visit" sounded suspiciously like "just a little hike." He quickly weighed the risks (an unknown island, a journey across deep, dark waters) against the potential benefits (a supposedly helpful friend, more suspects to investigate). And, of course, Mom and Dad were on Porpoise Island, so they'd be close by if anything went wrong.

Which raised an important question. "Should we tell Mom and Dad where we're going?" he asked. "They'd probably want to know."

"We could," said Grandpa. "But we'd have to tell them about the bees."

"Mom would worry," said Lizzie. "She might even want to come with us." She glanced at Mayhem in her backpack, and Leo guessed she was imagining what Mom and Dad would do if they saw her traveling with a kitten. "Could we not tell them? I mean, not yet?"

Grandpa looked at Leo, who looked back at Porpoise Island. Going there without telling Mom and Dad felt awfully irresponsible.

But as he gazed out at the island and the ocean rippling around it, that strange new feeling came back to him. Once again he felt bold and capable and maybe even a tiny bit adventurous.

He imagined the look on Mom and Dad's faces when he told them how he'd helped find Grandma's bees and brought them home.

"How about we don't tell them *yet*," he said. "Unless we need to. Then we'll tell them for sure."

Grandpa nodded. "All right. If we need to, we will. All in favor?" He looked at Lizzie.

"Aye!" she shouted. "To Porpoise Island!"

CHAPTER 13

They jogged down the mountain, hopped into the truck and sped back to Grandpa's to pack for Porpoise Island. Unsure how long the "quick visit" would actually last (Grandpa was vague on the details), Leo packed pajamas for himself and for Lizzie, plus a flashlight and his phone charger. Lizzie grabbed her drawing pencils and two cans of sardines for Mayhem. Grandpa took nothing but *Everything Bees*.

Both Leo and Lizzie were hungry, but there was no time for snacking, and, according to Grandpa, the ferry had a café on board. Within twenty minutes, they were back on the road, heading for the ferry terminal at Grandpa's usual speed. They pulled up to the ticket booth just in time to make the three o'clock sailing.

"Impeccable timing as always, Sam," the ticket seller commented as she handed him his ticket. "But don't you hate Porpoise Island?"

"I don't hate all of—" he began, then he shook his head. "Never mind." He grabbed his ticket and drove on.

"How does she know that?" Lizzie asked as they joined the cars and trucks lining up for the ferry.

"Small island, small world," said Grandpa. "People know things."

"So what do you hate about Porpoise Island?" Leo asked as they drove aboard the ferry and parked on the bottom deck of the boat.

"For one thing, there are too many people," said Grandpa. "Tourists especially. It used to be a nice, quiet island, but now it's all hotels and shops. Do you know, in some places you actually have to *pay* for parking?"

Leo recalled him mentioning something about unpaid parking tickets, but before he could ask more, Lizzie cut in.

"Can we go explore, Grandpa? I didn't get to last time we took the ferry because I was asleep."

"Sure, go ahead," he said, unbuckling his seat belt. "But come straight back when you hear the captain announce that we're nearing Porpoise Harbor. And remember where we parked. If there's one thing islanders hate, it's waiting to get off the boat because someone can't find their car."

Leo hadn't considered this potential risk. "You're not coming with us?"

"Nah," said Grandpa. "Oh, and pets aren't allowed up on deck."

"Aw, that's not fair." Lizzie pouted. "Mayhem wants to explore too."

"She'll be fine here with Grandpa," Leo assured her.

"Or just take her with you and keep her hidden." Grandpa pulled his hat down over his eyes.

"Wait, what?" Leo was alarmed. *That's* not a good idea!"

"Oh, I think it's a *great* idea!" Lizzie fastened Mayhem's leash to her collar, then tucked her into her jacket. "Let's go, Leo! Adventure awaits!" She leaped out of the truck.

"Wait, I—"

But before he could list the many things that could go wrong, she skipped off toward the stairs. He tossed a glare at Grandpa, then hurried after her.

"Come on, Leo!" Lizzie yelled over her shoulder, startling a woman climbing the stairs beside her. "Let's go see the ocean!"

"Little girl!" the woman scolded. But Lizzie didn't even pause. When she reached the top of the stairs, she took off running.

"Sorry," Leo said to the woman as he passed her. "She's new here."

At the top of the stairs, the wind off the water hit him square in the face, and a salty tang rushed up his nose. He stopped and looked around, shading his eyes from the sun. The deck spanned the length of the boat and was lined with benches and tables where passengers sat reading newspapers and sipping coffees. Overhead, a flock of seabirds circled, screeching.

Then a horn blew, and the boat began to pull away from the dock. Leo grabbed a nearby railing, thinking about the deep, dark water churning beneath him. Did the ferry have emergency lifeboats? he wondered. He wished he knew where to find them.

"Leo!"

He looked around for Lizzie and saw her standing farther down the deck, pointing out to sea.

"Look! Look!"

He hurried over. "What are we looking at?"

"There!" She pointed again.

About a hundred feet away, something sliced through the surface of the water. "What was that?"

"I think it's a whale! No, *two* whales!" Lizzie shouted as another fin appeared beside the first.

"No way!"

And then, something truly amazing happened. A shiny, black tail emerged from the water and gave it a big, hard *SLAP*.

Lizzie screamed. A family standing nearby applauded. "Orcas!" someone cried.

"Oh wow!" Leo breathed. While exploring the ocean in *Neptune 3: The Deepest Dive*, he'd seen some incredible creatures, like a transparent octopus and a very creepy anglerfish. But seeing real-life orcas in the ocean was truly next-level. It was almost magical.

Just when he thought it couldn't get any better, a *whole orca* rose up out of the water. It twisted in the air and fell back into the sea with an enormous splash.

The passengers cheered. Leo joined in. Lizzie bounced up and down and threw her hands in the air.

And Mayhem chose that moment to escape.

She leaped up out of Lizzie's jacket and twisted in the air just like the orca had moments before. Except she landed neatly and silently on her small, spotted paws. She paused for just a moment before galloping off down the deck, her purple leash trailing behind her.

"Mayhem!" Lizzie gasped. She and Leo looked at each other in horror, then sprinted off after her.

"Get her, Leo, get her!" Lizzie puffed behind him.

"I'm *trying*!" he shouted. But like Lizzie had said, Mayhem was superfast—so fast that the other passengers didn't even notice as she darted between their legs.

The magical feeling had disappeared; all Leo felt was regret. Why hadn't he put his foot down when Grandpa suggested Lizzie take Mayhem exploring? He knew it would be a disaster! He *knew*!

"Adventurers!" he growled.

"Is that a *cat*?" someone asked as Leo ran by, but he didn't stop to answer. He kept his eyes on the runaway kitten who was now headed toward a large metal structure that held an inflatable boat over the side of the ferry. It was a lifeboat! Leo realized. At any other time, he would have been relieved to see it, but in this particular emergency, it was no help at all.

"Leo, what if she jumps?" Lizzie gasped.

Before he could reply, Mayhem stopped at the foot of the metal structure. She glanced back at them, and though Leo was no Pandora Ali, he knew exactly what Mayhem was thinking. She was going to jump up onto it.

He slowed to a jog, his brain filling with terrible possibilities. What if Mayhem made it onto the lifeboat? What if she punctured it with her razor-sharp claws? Or worse, what if—

Suddenly, a boy appeared out of nowhere. He rushed past Leo and dove for the leash a split second before Mayhem jumped. The boy held on tight, and Mayhem dropped back down to the deck.

Leo gaped. Lizzie shrieked. Mayhem howled with indignation as the boy picked her up and turned to face them, looking nearly as shocked as they were.

It was then that Leo recognized him. Or rather, he recognized the "Jacques of All Trades" logo on the boy's green hat. It was Jacques's nephew!

"You saved her!" Lizzie threw her arms around the boy. "Thank you thank you thank you!"

The boy handed Mayhem back to Lizzie. "She's really fast," he said, blushing under his cap.

"Superfast!" Lizzie agreed. "I almost called her Lightning." She patted Mayhem's head. The kitten hissed.

Leo wracked his brain, trying to remember the boy's name, which Sofi had definitely mentioned. Was it Sandy? Samuel?

"Sawyer!" someone shouted.

Sawyer—that was it. Leo turned to see Sofi herself running their way.

"That was incredible!" she panted. "I was in the café getting a milkshake when I saw Mayhem run past the window—I recognized her right away. And then you all went running after her! It was like a scene out of a movie," she marveled. "Sawyer, you're a hero!"

Sawyer shook his head but looked pleased.

"You are," Leo insisted. "You saved Mayhem—and us."

"Seriously," Sofi agreed. "The no-pets-on-deck rule is no joke. Also, Bruno's serving milkshakes in the café today. You probably shouldn't let him see you." She lowered her voice. "He knows who hit his car last night."

Leo's stomach dropped. "He does?"

"Everyone knows," Sofi said matter-of-factly.

Sawyer nodded. "I heard about it too."

"Oh no," Leo moaned.

"Pets are only allowed on the car deck. I'll take you back down." Sofi motioned for them all to follow her down the deck. The orcas had long since disappeared, and the passengers had gone back to reading their newspapers and sipping coffee in the sun.

"So you're both going to Porpoise Island?" Lizzie asked Sofi and Sawyer. "How come?"

"A kid in our class who lives on Porpoise is having a birthday party tomorrow," she replied. "My mom's girlfriend lives on Porpoise too, so we're staying with her for the weekend. Tonight we're going to make pizza and watch movies."

"Fun!" said Lizzie.

"My uncle was going to Porpoise today, so I'm getting a ride with him," Sawyer said. "He'll bring me to the party tomorrow after we make some deliveries and pick up building supplies."

It didn't sound nearly as fun as a pizza-and-movie night, but Leo nodded politely.

"Did I mention Sawyer's an amazing woodworker?" Sofi said as she led them down the stairs to the car deck. "He built a hutch for our class's rabbits last year. All by himself!"

"Rabbits?" Lizzie gasped. "You have *rabbits in your class*?"

She and Sawyer nodded.

"That's amazing!" Lizzie marveled. "Do you make scratch pads for cats, Sawyer?"

He shook his head. "Should I?"

"Definitely," said Lizzie. "People pay a lot of money for them. Cat trees too. Check out PandoraAli.com if you want ideas," she advised.

Sawyer promised he'd look into it, then excused himself to go find his uncle.

"Thanks again for saving Mayhem!" Lizzie shouted after him.

"I guess you haven't found the bees yet," Sofi said as they continued on.

"Not yet," said Leo. And because Lizzie's question about scratch pads had jogged his memory, he asked, "Do you know if my grandma labeled her beehives alphabetically? Like with a letter on each hive?"

Sofi thought for a moment. "I don't think so. Some beekeepers paint their names or initials on their hives, though. My mom uses a bee-shaped stamp on hers. It's cute, but I think a GPS tracker would be more useful. Have you seen those?"

Leo shook his head.

"They're little devices you attach to your hives, and if the hives go missing, the trackers send a signal to your phone and tell you where they are. Isn't that great?"

Leo nodded, wishing Grandma had thought to install GPS trackers on her hives. But then, they wouldn't have been much use since Grandpa didn't have a cell phone.

"Why did you ask about labeling?" asked Sofi.

Leo told her about the scratch pad they'd found on Heron Mountain. "Grandpa was investigating Jacques's place," he admitted. "But he didn't find anything. Maybe don't tell Sawyer. Does he live there too?"

Sofi shook her head. "Sawyer's mom owns the hardware store in town, and they have a cute apartment above it. Anyway, I won't tell him." She tapped her chin thoughtfully. "So Jacques isn't the thief. And it's not Bruno or Marguerite, and obviously it's not my mom. It's probably not the other Bumblers either since they were Evelyn's friends."

Leo recalled Jin's memorial mural and agreed it was unlikely.

"So who's left?"

"Grandpa said there are lots of beekeepers on Porpoise Island, so we're going there to investigate," he told her.

"Apparently he has a friend who can help us."

"Sam has a *friend*?" Sofi looked shocked.

"That's what I said," said Lizzie.

"Wow. Who is it?"

Leo tried to recall. "Mo, I think?"

"Hmm." She looked thoughtful. Then her eyes grew wide. "You don't mean Big Mo, do you?"

"Um . . . I'm not sure?" Grandpa hadn't mentioned anything about Mo's size.

Sofi stopped beside a van and motioned for them to step closer. "Listen, Big Mo is a criminal! He spent time in prison!"

"What?" Leo squawked.

"A criminal?" Lizzie whispered.

Sofi nodded. "I mean, I've never actually met him. I've never even seen him, to be honest. But I've heard things."

"Maybe there's more than one Mo on the island?" Leo suggested.

"Or maybe Mo went to prison for something not-so-bad," Lizzie suggested. "Like in that movie we saw about the dad who stole food to feed his family. Remember, Leo? Maybe that's what Mo did."

"Maybe," Sofi said, but she sounded doubtful.

Leo felt queasy. Could Grandpa's only friend really be a criminal?

"Let's trade numbers." Sofi pulled her phone out of her pocket. "If you ever need help, you can text me."

Leo grabbed his phone and opened his contacts list.

He added Sofi's number as an emergency contact, very much hoping he wouldn't need it.

"Is there anything else we should know about the island?" he asked. "Like, are there feral goats there too?"

He'd meant it as a joke, to lighten the mood. But Sofi looked serious. "No," she said. "But there is Penelope."

"Penelope?"

"She's a wild pig."

"A wild pig?!" Leo cried. "Like in *Applewood Acres 2: Hog Wild*?"

"Exactly." She nodded. "Except, well, she's real. She invades people's gardens, breaks up picnics, chases puppies . . ."

Lizzie yelped and wrapped her arms around Mayhem.

"You've got to be kidding me," Leo moaned. Had he known there were so many risks on Porpoise Island, he never would have agreed to go.

"But you probably won't even see her," Sofi assured them. "It's a big island—five times the size of Heron Island. I've been there hundreds of times, and I've only seen Penelope once, from far away. And it could have been a cow—I'm not a hundred percent sure."

"Really?" asked Lizzie.

"Really," said Sofi. "I'd be *way* more worried about visiting Big Mo than meeting Penelope. Now *that's* something to worry about."

CHAPTER 14

Leo took Sofi's advice. He worried for the rest of the ferry ride, which he spent in the truck listening to Grandpa snore and Mayhem claw her scratch pad while Lizzie cheered her on. He was still worrying as they drove off the boat and into Porpoise Harbor, which turned out to be a real town, with a grocery store, community center and streets lined with shops and restaurants.

"There's a place called Porpoise Pizzeria." Lizzie leaned across Leo to point out the window. "And there's Sweet Nothings Ice Cream Parlor . . . Sushi-to-Go . . . Jaspreet's Tandoori Kitchen . . ."

"We can read, Lizzie," Leo told her.

"And there's a sign for the Porpoise Island Spa and Resort! Look, Grandpa!"

"We're not going anywhere near that place," Grandpa grumped.

"There's a sign for a petting zoo," she went on, unde-
terred. "And that one says 'Wine-Tasting Tours.'"

Grandpa scoffed. "Now there's a waste of money."

"Or we could do a cheese-tasting tour." Lizzie pointed
to another sign. "I like cheese!"

He scoffed again.

"Whale-watching tours!" Lizzie cried as they sped
through the town. "That'd be fun!"

Scoff, scoff, scoff.

Leo wasn't sure which was more annoying: Lizzie's
need to read every single sign aloud or Grandpa's need
to scoff at them. He tried to tune them out and focus on
his most pressing worry: that Grandpa was taking them to
visit a convicted criminal.

Maybe, he reminded himself. It was also possible that
Sofi was wrong, though she didn't seem like someone who
was wrong very often.

He knew he couldn't ask Grandpa outright. Grandpa
would want to know how Leo heard about Mo's question-
able past, and Leo would have to admit that Béatriz's
daughter had told him, and that would only cause more
trouble.

He decided instead to try some opening questions,
which he'd learned about playing *Peregrine Peabody:
Private Eye*. Opening questions were questions that got the
interview subject talking so they'd be comfortable when
you asked them more hard-hitting questions later.

He began with: "So, Grandpa, where does Mo live?"

"East end of the island," said Grandpa. "Can you find that on your phone?"

Leo nodded and opened it. Before they'd parted, Sofi had made him another map, this time of Porpoise Island. He'd found an outlet to charge his phone and used the ferry's extremely weak Wi-Fi signal to download the map.

"Look for Desolation Road."

"*Desolation Road?*"

"Yep."

Leo found it easily, as it was the only road on the east end of the island. "Is there another town around there?"

Grandpa shook his head. "Nothing but forest on that side of the island. Mo's a bit of a hermit."

Leo bit his lip. This was not comforting news.

The farther they drove from Porpoise Harbor, the fewer houses they saw, and the more the island looked like the one they'd left: all twisty roads and shadowy forests and ivy climbing over everything, like the plant in *Green Thumb* that snacked on human flesh. Leo shuddered, then remembered another worrisome thing about the island.

"Have you heard anything about a wild pig on Porpoise Island?" he asked, this time very much hoping Grandpa would scoff.

But Grandpa nodded seriously. "You mean Penelope. She's a real menace."

Leo's stomach sank. "Really?"

"I've never seen her myself, but Mo has, several times. Apparently, she's enormous and getting bigger by the day."

Leo clutched his seat belt. "Penelope lives near Mo's place?"

"Maybe." Grandpa turned off the main road and onto a smaller one, heading deeper into the woods. "She gets around."

For perhaps the first time in his life, Leo had no desire to ask any more questions.

It took nearly half an hour to drive across the island, and Lizzie kept a running commentary on everything she saw out the window: a field of cows, an apple orchard, a stand selling fresh eggs, a tree decorated with shoes, a fence lined with teapots.

Just when Leo was dangerously close to snapping, Grandpa turned onto a tiny, gravel road that plunged down a steep hill. It felt like they were being swallowed up by the forest. "Are we almost there?" Leo asked, dreading the answer.

"It's right up ahead," said Grandpa.

"This is so spooky." As usual, Lizzie sounded more excited than concerned.

Squinting out the window, Leo saw nothing but trees. It was the perfect place for a criminal. No one would find him—or his victims—in the deep, dark woods.

His heart was racing by the time Mo's place came into view. It was made of dark wood like the trees surrounding it, and its roof was covered in moss so thick it looked like a creature itself. Like the Green Thumb that snacked on human—

Stop it! Leo scolded himself.

"Mo bought this place when it was just a shack and added onto it over the years," Grandpa said, parking in front of the house. "It's a great little place. No one bothers you here."

And no one will find you if something awful happens, Leo thought as he slid out of the truck, followed by Lizzie and Mayhem. He took note of possible escape routes as he climbed the steps to the front door. There weren't many options, with only one road out and the forest closing on all sides. Possibly he and Lizzie could climb a tree, though he'd never climbed one before and wasn't sure how.

Grandpa knocked on the door, then waited. No one answered. Leo crossed his fingers that no one was home and they'd have to leave.

But then he heard footsteps approaching.

Big footsteps. *Heavy* footsteps.

He stepped closer to Lizzie and held his breath as the door clicked, then slowly opened, revealing the largest man Leo had ever seen. He looked to be nearly seven feet tall, with a shiny, bald head and arms covered in tattoos—Leo could make out a dragon, a shark and something that looked like a cupcake but almost certainly wasn't. The man wore a canvas apron that was smeared with some-thing red. Something that looked suspiciously like blood.

Leo reached for Lizzie's hand, ready to make a break for the forest. But then Grandpa threw his hands in the air and shouted, "Corny!"

Corny?

The man's face broke into an enormous smile. "Sam!" He flung the door open wide, swept Grandpa into a hug and *picked him up off the ground*!

Leo's mouth fell open.

If that weren't shocking enough, Grandpa proceeded to laugh! Not just a chuckle, but a great, big belly laugh.

"What's going on?" Lizzie whispered.

Leo had no idea.

The man set Grandpa back down on the steps, and Grandpa patted the shark tattoo on his arm. "Good to see you, kiddo!" he declared, though the man was clearly not a kid. "These are my grandchildren, Leo and Lizzie. This is Cornelius, but we call him Corny."

Corny extended a hand, and Leo took it hesitantly. It was surprisingly soft. "But . . . um, what about Mo?"

No sooner had he asked than a tiny, elderly woman barreled through the doorway and onto the steps. "Where have you been, you big galoot?" she demanded. "I haven't heard from you in months!"

Grandpa laughed (Laughed! Again!) and threw his arms around her. "Mo!"

"Wait, *what*?" said Leo.

"I thought Mo was a man!" cried Lizzie. Leo shushed her, though of course he'd thought so too. Hadn't Sofi said so?

"And this must be Leo and Lizzie." Mo turned to them. She had short, silver hair and pale blue eyes, and she was wearing a plaid shirt that looked like it belonged to someone ten times her size—quite possibly Corny. "My goodness, I've heard so much about you two!"

"You . . . have?" said Leo.

"I'm Mo." She shook their hands. "Maureen, actually, but no one calls me that."

"*You're* Big Mo?" said Lizzie.

Leo elbowed her.

"Now where did you hear that name?" asked Grandpa.

"But you're so little," Lizzie persisted.

"Lizzie," Leo hissed.

Mo winked. "What I lack in size, I make up for in personality. Right, Corny?"

Corny laughed. "No kidding, Mom."

"Come in, come in!" She ushered them inside. "Corny's making us a delicious dinner. We've been feasting like royalty since he got back from Sweden last month."

"I can't wait!" Grandpa bounded through the door. Leo followed, dizzy with questions.

The inside of Mo's house looked nothing like the outside. It was cozy and warm with big windows looking out onto the forest, which didn't look nearly as creepy from inside. There were reading nooks in every corner, filled with pillows and piled with books. It felt like a big tree house.

A black-and-white dog with long, floppy ears was lounging on a carpet near the fireplace, undisturbed by their arrival. "That's Waffle," said Mo. "He's old and doesn't move much these days, but he's very friendly. And he loves cats," she added to Lizzie, who had Mayhem in her arms.

Lizzie set Mayhem down but held on to her leash. As they watched, Mayhem walked right up to Waffle and gave him a soft tap on the nose. Waffle rolled over and licked Mayhem's chin. Within minutes she was lying beside him, chewing on his ear.

"Huckleberry soda, anyone?" Corny offered. "I just made it, with fresh berries—hence this mess." He gestured to his apron. Then he poured them each a tall glass of cold, fizzy juice. It was wonderfully sweet and tart—possibly the best drink Leo had ever had.

They sat down at the kitchen table, and Corny whirled around the kitchen, slicing and sautéing ingredients for dinner and telling them all about his time in Stockholm, where he'd worked as a chef in a restaurant.

"A *Michelin-starred* restaurant," Mo added as she sipped her soda.

"Is that fancy?" asked Lizzie.

"Very! And now he wants to open a restaurant here, serving dishes made with all local ingredients. Heaven knows the tourists will pay for it." Mo gave Grandpa a knowing look.

Grandpa scoffed. Then Mo scoffed. Then they scoffed again, together.

Leo was beginning to understand why they were friends.

What he couldn't understand was how Mo could possibly be a criminal. Sofi must have been wrong, he decided. There were probably two Mos on Porpoise Island.

He drank his huckleberry soda and watched Corny twirl around the kitchen like a dancer, but wielding a chef's knife. He told them he was preparing Coho salmon on a bed of seaweed he'd harvested himself, plus chanterelle mushrooms he'd foraged in the forest and a huckleberry mousse for dessert. Leo had never eaten any of these things, but to his surprise, he couldn't wait to try them.

The biggest surprise, however, was Grandpa himself. It was like he'd become a different person the moment Corny had opened the door. He was smiling, laughing, even *guffawing*. Leo barely recognized him.

"This huckleberry soda is excellent, Corny," Grandpa said, raising his glass. "It reminds me of the time we took you and Sarah berry picking. Remember that? You couldn't have been more than six years old."

Corny grinned. "I still have the photo Mom took of us, completely covered in berry juice."

"Sarah was so upset—she loved her clothes and hated berry picking," laughed Mo.

"Hang on," Leo interjected. "You mean Sarah as in *Mom*? You know her?"

"Of course!" said Mo. "We go way back. Sarah and Corny went to school together."

"Really?" Leo had never heard Mom mention Mo or Corny. It didn't surprise him, however, that she'd hated berry picking and getting her clothes dirty.

Dinner was more delicious than Leo could have ever imagined—he would have happily eaten Corny's huckleberry mousse every day for the rest of his life. It was so good that he barely noticed Lizzie's mouth noises. In fact, he barely noticed Lizzie at all until she finished her dessert and turned to Mo. "So are you really a criminal?" she asked.

"Lizzie!" Leo exclaimed.

Grandpa's eyes grew wide. Corny stood and began clearing the table.

"What?" Lizzie looked around. "I just want to know."

Leo groaned softly. It had all been going so well.

"It's fine." Mo patted Lizzie's hand. "I can understand your curiosity. And I'm not a criminal—not now, anyway. I did make some mistakes, but it was a long time ago—nearly fifty years."

Leo sucked in his breath. So it was true!

"But how did you know about that?" Grandpa looked confounded.

Lizzie glanced at Leo.

He gulped. "We . . . um . . ."

"No matter," Mo said firmly. "Folks around here talk a lot—we know that, don't we, Sam? It's not important. Now, who wants tea?"

"I'm on it!" Corny called, and he began to tell them about the wild mint he'd picked and dried for tea. Leo suspected Corny was trying to change the subject, and he was glad for it.

Of course, now he had more questions than ever. How could Mo, who seemed so kind and caring, be a former criminal? And what had she done? Slammed into a car and driven away without leaving a note? Trespassed on someone's property? Or something worse?

He pondered this as the adults talked and the forest grew dark outside the windows. Lizzie began to nod off beside him. Over by the fireplace, Waffle was still lounging on the floor, Mayhem tucked under his chin.

"Late, isn't it?" Mo stretched and yawned. "Obviously you'll stay here tonight. There's a bed for you kids in the den." She led them to a room beside the kitchen, where a big mattress lay on the floor, covered with a quilt. Lizzie flopped down without even changing into her pajamas. By the time Leo had changed and joined her, she was already fast asleep.

He tucked himself in and listened to Grandpa and Mo talking in the kitchen, recalling a time when they got stuck on a mountain in a snowstorm. Leo couldn't make out the details of the story because Grandpa and Mo were laughing so hard.

It made Leo wonder if he really knew Grandpa at all. He definitely didn't know him the way Mo did. And if Mo knew a different side of Grandpa, Grandma must have too.

Was that why Grandpa was so happy at Mo's? Because he was with people who knew him?

Questions swarmed in Leo's brain. But the bed was soft and the quilt was heavy and the room smelled like a bonfire, in a nice, cozy way. And before he could even begin to sort through the questions, he was sleeping as soundly as an Adventurer.

CHAPTER 15

The next morning, Leo sat at the kitchen table and watched Corny make pancakes studded with thimble-berries, which of course he'd picked himself. Lizzie was outside helping Mayhem hunt for spiders. And Grandpa and Mo were sitting by the living room window, sipping coffee and discussing next steps in the search for the missing bees. Mo thought Grandpa ought to visit a farmers' market at the south end of the island, where several bee-keepers sold their honey.

"Just don't go storming in and accusing them all of stealing," she warned him.

"I wouldn't do that!" he protested.

Mo snorted. "Oh, please!"

Leo was about to offer that he knew a thing or two about interviewing suspects when he heard Lizzie shriek.

He hurried for the door with Mo close behind. They found Lizzie standing at the edge of the forest, staring up a tree the height of a six-story building. "Mayhem!" she yelled.

Leo ran over. "What happened?"

"She slipped out of her collar!" Lizzie held up Mayhem's collar, which was still fastened to her leash. "And look!" She pointed up at the tree, and Leo squinted until he spotted the kitten, perched on a branch about twenty feet off the ground.

"Oh no!" Mayhem wasn't just an Adventurer—she was an escape artist!

"Mayhem, come down!" Lizzie called, waving her arms.

"She's a long way up." Mo tsked. "I'll go get a ladder. Maybe Corny can help, though he's never been good with heights."

"No need!" Grandpa stomped out of the house, rolling up the sleeves of his jacket. He pulled his hat down on his head, then on second thought cast it aside. Flexing his fingers, he marched toward the tree.

"Sam, are you sure?" Mo sounded decidedly unsure. "You're not as spry as you used to be."

"What's he doing?" Leo asked. "He's not going to—"

She sighed. "Oh yes, he is."

Grandpa stopped at the base of the tree and let out a great, big grumble-huff. Then he bent his knees and jumped, grabbing the branch above his head.

Leo gasped.

"Classic Sam," Mo muttered as Grandpa swung himself up onto the branch, then reached for one above it.

"Whoa," Leo breathed. "Where did he learn to do *that*?"

"You know he used to be a tree topper, don't you?" said Mo. "He did this for nearly a decade. Except he had ropes securing him to the tree in case he fell."

"Really?" said Leo. "What's a tree topper?"

"Someone who climbs trees—often very tall trees—to cut off the tops so they can be felled. You didn't know he did that?"

He shook his head. He'd known that Grandpa had worked for a logging company, but he'd never thought to ask what that meant.

"This was a long time ago," said Mo. "Back before your mom was born. You hear that, Sam?" she shouted. "It was *a long time ago*! You'd better be careful!"

"I'll be fine!" he hollered back, now more than ten feet off the ground. "The trick is to brace one foot against a rough area of the trunk," he told them as he climbed higher. "Push into the tree, not down, or your foot will slip."

"You'd better not slip!" Mo threatened. "I don't want to drag you to the hospital!"

"This is bananas," Leo whispered.

"He's almost there!" Lizzie squealed. "He's going to save Mayhem!"

"As long as she doesn't climb any higher," Mo grumbled.

146

Thankfully, Mayhem didn't move. And as they watched, Grandpa pulled himself up to the kitten's perch, steadied himself, then grabbed her by the scruff of her neck.

"Oh no you don't!" Grandpa grunted. The branches shook, and a few cones tumbled to the ground. A moment later, he shouted, "Got 'er! Coming down!"

Lizzie danced over to the base of the tree, cheering, "Grand-PA! Grand-PA!"

"Bananas." Leo shook his head.

"This is nothing," Mo told him. "Sam once rescued a deer that fell through the ice of a lake. He lay down flat on the ice so he wouldn't fall in too, then grabbed the deer by its antlers and hauled it out." She laughed. "He's always loved animals—can't bear to see them in distress."

Leo stared at her. "Seriously?!" That sounded like something Pandora Ali would do. "Grandpa?"

"Oh yes." She chuckled.

"I can't believe it," Leo murmured. Clearly his suspicions were correct: he didn't know Grandpa well at all.

And, he thought as he looked over at Mo, I know even less about her.

"You look like you have questions," she observed. "Sam says you often do."

He flushed, remembering Grandpa demanding if he ever *stopped* asking questions.

"Questions are good," she added quickly. "I'm a curious person too."

For once, he knew exactly which question he wanted to ask. But he hesitated, unsure how she'd take it.

"Is it the question Lizzie asked last night?"

He nodded.

"I don't mind talking about it," Mo assured him. "It was a long time ago, and I've learned a lot since then. You see, when I was in my early twenties, I landed an excellent job. It involved investigating companies to figure out whether they were committing fraud. Do you know what fraud is?"

Leo nodded. He'd learned about fraud in *Peregrine Peabody, Private Eye 2: Skeletons in the Closet.* "It's when you lie or deceive someone, usually for money."

"Right," said Mo. "I was kind of like a detective, searching for corporate crime."

"Neat," said Leo.

"To make a long story short, one day I found some incriminating evidence. But my boss asked me—told me, really—to cover it up. I was young and not very brave, so I did what I was told. But eventually someone found out, and my boss and I got charged with withholding evidence. That's a pretty big crime."

"Oh!" Leo tried to wrap his head around this information. "Wow."

She nodded. "I'll always regret it, not least of all because I could never go back to that job, and I loved it. It was the perfect job for me."

Leo thought about all the time Dad had spent searching for his own perfect job. Apparently, they could be hard to find. "So what did you do instead?"

She looked over at Grandpa, who was climbing down slowly, mindful of the kitten in his jacket. "I decided to do things that scared me, to make me a braver person. I fought forest fires for a time. I climbed mountains to measure the depth of glaciers. And I worked as a search and rescue paramedic. That's actually how I met your Grandpa: he fell out of a tree in a remote logging camp, and I had to fly in, collect him and bring him to the hospital. He was the grumpiest person I'd ever met." She smiled. "We became fast friends."

Leo could see why. "You must be an Adventurer too then," he said.

"An Adventurer?"

"Like Grandpa and Lizzie," he said. "They're Adventurers. According to Fatefinder.com."

She looked at him curiously.

"It's a website with personality quizzes that help people find their perfect jobs," he explained. "My dad's really into it."

"I see," she said. "You must be an Adventurer too then."

"Me? Oh no!" He shook his head. "I'm an Auditor."

She raised an eyebrow. "You don't sound too happy about that."

Leo admitted he wasn't thrilled.

Mo paused for a moment, then said, "Come with me." She led him over to a big fallen log, which someone—quite possibly Mo herself—had carved into a bench. She sat down and patted the seat beside her. "Tell me more about this Auditor business."

He sat down beside her. And although he barely knew her, he found himself wanting to tell her about it—possibly because she'd just shared something important about herself. So he told her all about Problem Solvers and Counselors, Adventurers and Auditors, and how he was destined to sit at a desk and check people's tax returns, and how the thought of it made him despair.

When he was done, Mo stayed quiet for a long moment. "We love to put labels on people, don't we?" she said finally. "I think we do it to make people seem less complicated, so we can predict what they're going to do. But people *are* complicated, and that's a good thing. We're all delightfully complicated."

Leo nodded, though he wasn't quite sure he understood.

"And labels limit us, don't they?" she went on. "They can make us feel small."

That he understood perfectly. He nodded again.

"The fact is, Leo, no one knows you better than you know yourself. You can't let other people—or companies, for that matter—tell you who you are or what you should do."

It made sense when she said it like that. "But . . . what if you don't know what you should do?"

She hummed thoughtfully. "Then I guess you start exploring. You can explore close to home by trying new things and talking to new people. And asking lots of questions, of course—you're already good at that. Maybe someday you'll explore farther afield too."

Leo thought about Mom standing on a subway platform in rush hour, knowing she'd found her forever home. That was an Adventurer thing to do, he realized. Even though she was a Counselor according to Fatefinder.com.

"And don't rush it," Mo added. "Good explorations take time."

He liked the sound of that. "Okay."

"For what it's worth," she added, "your grandpa says you have great detective skills. He says you're always thinking ahead, one step ahead of everyone else."

"He said that?" Leo was shocked.

She nodded. "He said that if he had a very important mission, he'd want you to come along."

Leo remembered his first morning at Grandpa's house, when Grandpa had asked him to come tell the bees about Grandma. He *had* said something like that.

"Really?"

"Of course! He thinks the world of you!"

"Him?" Leo pointed at Grandpa, who was nearing the base of the tree, where Lizzie was turning cartwheels. "But he's so . . . Grandpa."

Mo laughed. "He sure is. And don't forget, your grandma was one in a million. Even I liked her, and I don't like many people. Sam hasn't yet figured out how to live without her. But he'll get there, Leo. And you might find this hard to believe, but you're helping him."

He did find that hard to believe.

"Now, I'm going to finish my coffee." She stood up from the log bench and started toward the house, then stopped. "You know, I almost forgot an important part of my story."

"What's that?" asked Leo.

"Do you know what my job title was, when I was fighting corporate crime?"

"Um . . . corporate crime fighter?"

She grinned. "Investigative forensic auditor."

Leo's mouth fell open. "You were an *auditor*?"

"Sure was," said Mo. "It was a great job."

Before he could ask any more questions, Grandpa's boots hit the ground and Mayhem let out an offended cry. Grandpa pulled her out of his jacket and handed her to Lizzie.

Maybe it was because he was with friends who knew him, who found him delightfully complicated. Or maybe it was because he'd just rescued an animal in need. Whatever the reason, Grandpa looked like a light had been lit deep inside him. He practically sparkled. He beamed.

Leo couldn't help but beam back.

CHAPTER 16

They breakfasted on thimbleberry pancakes drizzled with syrup that Corny had tapped from local maple trees. Once everyone was full, Leo, Lizzie and Grandpa packed up their things and got ready to leave.

Mo and Corny stood on the doorstep of the moss-covered cabin, waving as they piled into the truck. Grandpa tooted the horn and backed up the driveway, and Lizzie and Leo waved until they could no longer see their new friends through the trees. The forest didn't seem nearly as scary now as it had when they arrived. Leo would never have guessed he'd be sad to leave it.

But by the time they reached the main road, his sadness had mostly disappeared. The sky above them was a cloudless blue, and the air was warm and smelled like the ocean. They were bound for the farmers' market at the south end of the island, where local beekeepers would be selling their honey.

"We're off to find the bees! We're on a big adventure," Lizzie sang to Mayhem, who was now traveling in a crate at her feet. Corny had found it in Mo's garage—apparently Waffle used it when he was a tiny puppy. Corny insisted they take it, that Mayhem would be safer traveling that way.

"Oh!" Leo cried. "We're on a *sting*!" He laughed—he couldn't believe he'd never thought of it before. "A sting is like an operation to catch someone committing a crime," he explained to Lizzie. "Isn't that perfect?"

She gave him a funny look.

"Get it?" he said. "It's—"

"A pun," she finished. She looked over at Grandpa, who'd suddenly gone quiet and still.

Leo gulped, cursing himself for forgetting Grandpa's one rule. "I'm sorry, Grandpa. I—"

"A sting!" Grandpa slapped the steering wheel, making him jump. "It's a sting! Now *that's* a good one!"

"It . . . it is?" asked Leo.

"The big sting. Why didn't I think of that?" Grandpa threw back his head and guffawed.

Leo looked at Lizzie, who shrugged. "It is a pretty good one," she agreed. "It's almost funny."

"It's a great one!" Grandpa declared. "I'd say it's . . . it's un-*bee*-lievably good!"

Leo's mouth fell open. Grandpa was punning!

"It's *bee*-autiful!" cried Lizzie.

Grandpa slapped the steering wheel again. "That's a good one too!"

"So wait—the ban on puns is over?" Leo asked. "Just like that?"

Grandpa nodded. "It's time. Because you know what a ban on puns is?"

"What?"

"PUN-ishment!" he roared. Lizzie doubled over laughing.

Leo had no idea what had brought on the sudden change, but he did have a brain full of puns waiting to be released. "You know, if we find the bees," he told them, "it'll create a real buzz around the island."

Lizzie and Grandpa snickered.

"But if we don't, that'll be a real *buzz*kill."

Grandpa groaned. "You know what we'll do if we find them?"

"What?"

"Throw a house-swarming party."

They laughed until their sides hurt and Grandpa had to pull over to wipe tears from his eyes. He blew his nose on a handkerchief, then sighed. "Evelyn loved puns, you know."

"She did?" said Lizzie.

He nodded. "They were her favorite thing. Or maybe her second-favorite thing, after the bees. When she passed away, I just couldn't stand to hear them. They weren't funny anymore—they were sad."

Leo remembered Mo saying that Grandpa hadn't yet figured out how to live without Grandma. He was about to offer that they could reinstate the ban on puns if it made things easier when Grandpa cleared his throat and continued.

"But just now, they made me happy again." He tucked his handkerchief away. "In fact, I had actually missed them." He paused, then shook his head and started the truck again. "Let's keep going."

He eased them back onto the road, and they punned some more as they drove. Lizzie rolled down her window, and a breeze blew in, carrying scents of the sea. Leo breathed in deeply and felt better than he had in days. They were on an adventure—a big sting. Maybe someone at the farmers' market would know about the bees. And if not, they'd just look someplace else.

"Hey, Grandpa." He turned to him. "Did you hear about the bees that went to California?"

Grandpa rubbed his chin. "Were they on their honeymoon?"

Leo snorted. Then he told Grandpa everything he'd learned about Californian almond groves and the millions of bees that traveled across the country every year to pollinate them. He told him about the bees that had gone missing in Montana, snatched by sticky-fingered thieves.

Grandpa listened thoughtfully. "California, hey? Well, let's search Porpoise Island first. If we don't find them here, we'll consider it as a next step. It would be a very long drive, you know."

"We're up for it," said Lizzie.

Leo agreed. He could see it now: the three of them (four including Mayhem), road-tripping all the way to California.

He felt a warmth in his chest, as if a light had been lit deep inside him.

Suddenly, Grandpa snapped his fingers. "Wait a second. That's it!"

"What's it?"

"You just reminded me. Last spring, a couple that runs an orchard here called Evelyn and asked if they could borrow her hives. They'd planted a new crop of trees—hazelnuts, I think—and wanted to make sure they got pollinated. Evelyn said no—she thought the move between islands would be too stressful for the bees. And those orchardists weren't happy." Grandpa shook his head. "I had forgotten about that until just now."

"Wow," said Leo. "They might actually have a plausible motive for stealing the bees."

"We should go investigate," said Lizzie.

Leo pulled out his phone and tapped open his map. "Where do they live?"

"Look for Cascadia Farm," said Grandpa.

Leo searched the map and found it easily. "It's not too far. Maybe twenty minutes away."

"All right, we'll go there first," said Grandpa. "If we don't find anything, we'll try the market. But I have a pretty strong feeling about this."

Leo nodded. So did he.

"We'll have to stop for gas first, though." Grandpa pointed at a gas station up ahead. He pulled into the lot and parked beside a pump, then took out his wallet and gave Leo a few bills. "Go inside and get me some black licorice—the salty kind," he said. "And get any snacks you want too."

"Snacks!" Lizzie cheered. "I'll bring Mayhem—I bet she wants a break." She pulled Mayhem out of her crate and tucked her into her backpack. Then she and Leo went inside to survey the snacks.

"Leo, look!" she exclaimed. "Tropical Hawaiian potato chips! What do you think those taste like?"

"I don't know, but look at this." He held up a candy bar called Choco-chomps, which he'd never seen before.

"This place is amazing," said Lizzie. "I've never seen so many kinds of candy."

They'd only just begun to narrow down their options when the bell on the door jangled and Grandpa came running in.

"I have to go back," he puffed. "I forgot my book!"

"Huh?" Leo looked up from the three chocolate bars he'd been considering.

"*Everything Bees*! I left it at Mo's." Grandpa pulled at his hair.

"Do you need it right now?" asked Leo.

"It's Evelyn's. I can't leave it behind." Grandpa looked at the chocolate bars in Leo's hands and the five bags of chips Lizzie was holding. "You two stay here and pay for your snacks. I'll be back in fifteen minutes. Okay?"

Leo nodded. Grandpa turned and ran for the door.

After several minutes' debate, Leo and Lizzie settled on the tropical Hawaiian chips, a bag of sour jelly beans, the Choco-chomps and Grandpa's salted black licorice, which they agreed sounded terrible—the kind of snack you'd eat only in an emergency situation. They paid the cashier and went back outside. Grandpa had not yet returned.

"Can we open the jelly beans?" asked Lizzie.

"Let's wait until he gets back." Leo hadn't checked his phone when Grandpa left, but he guessed he'd been gone about fifteen minutes. "He won't be much longer."

They waited five minutes, then five minutes more. Lizzie let Mayhem out of her backpack to explore a patch of grass.

"Where do you think he is?" she wondered.

"He's on his way," Leo assured her. Though he *was* taking a surprisingly long time.

"Hey, look!" Lizzie pointed to a truck pulling into the lot.

"That truck's green." Leo sighed. "Grandpa's is brown—you know that."

"*Duh*," she retorted. "It's Jacques and Sawyer!"

159

"It is?" he squinted. "Oh yeah!"

Jacques parked next to a gas pump, and Sawyer tumbled out the passenger door. He ran straight for them. "Leo! Lizzie! What's going on?"

"We're just waiting for Grandpa," Lizzie told him. "He went back to Mo's to get his book."

Sawyer stopped, looking confused.

"He'll be back soon," Leo added, though he was feeling less and less confident about that.

"I . . . um . . . don't think he will," said Sawyer.

"What? Why?"

He swallowed. "We just saw your Grandpa on the road, maybe ten minutes ago. He'd been pulled over by the police."

"No!" Lizzie gasped.

"Wait, *what*?" Leo cried. "Why?"

"I don't know," said Sawyer. "But he might be in trouble. They were taking him away in their car."

CHAPTER 17

"They were WHAT?" Leo couldn't believe his ears.

"GRANDPA!" Lizzie hollered, as if he might be able to hear her.

"He didn't look hurt, though," Sawyer added quickly. "I don't think he'd been in an accident."

"Sawyer!" Jacques shouted from the gas pump. "We have to go!"

Sawyer waved at his uncle, then turned back to Leo and Lizzie. "He's dropping me off at the birthday party. But maybe we could give you a ride somewhere? I'd have to ask Jacques, but he'll probably say yes."

Jacques blared the truck horn.

Sawyer winced. "I have to use the washroom. I'll be right back." He signaled to his uncle, then ran inside the gas station.

Leo turned to Lizzie, whose eyes were enormous. "Is Grandpa okay?" she whispered.

"I don't know," he said. "I hope so."

"Do you think . . ." She gulped. "They threw him in jail?"

"I doubt it," he said. "But I don't know that either."

"Will he come back?"

"Lizzie, I don't know!" Leo exclaimed, then forced himself to take a deep breath. Getting angry wasn't going to help.

She stamped her foot. "Well then, we need to go after him!"

"Okay, but we don't know where he went." Leo thought for a moment. "Was there a police station in Porpoise Harbor?"

She shrugged. "Why would I know?"

He stopped himself from reminding her that she'd insisted on reading every single sign they'd passed out loud. "If there's a police station on the island, it's probably in Porpoise Harbor. We could get them to drop us off there." He looked over at Jacques of All Trades. He didn't love the idea of asking him for a ride.

"Can we call Mo?" asked Lizzie.

"We don't have her number," said Leo. And then he remembered. "But I *do* have Sofi's number!"

"Text her! Text her!" Lizzie jumped up and down. Mayhem yelped in her backpack.

He pulled out his phone and began to compose a text.

Hi Sofi. It's Leo

"Hurry hurry hurry," Lizzie chanted.

"Right." He deleted all that and got straight to the point. **If someone got arrested on Porpoise Island, where would they end up?**

Seconds after he hit "send," Sofi's reply came through. **OMG WHO GOT ARRESTED? SAM???**

Did Grandpa actually get arrested? Leo wasn't even sure. **Maybe not,** he replied. **Maybe detained?** He'd heard that on TV once, but wasn't quite sure what it meant.

OMG, said Sofi's next message. **Let me think**

Leo waited. Lizzie bounced from one foot to the other.

There's a police station in Porpoise Harbor behind the community center. He must be there. I'll tell my mom. She'll take me!

Leo tried to imagine what Grandpa would do if Béatriz and Sofi showed up at the police station. **Maybe don't** he told her. **Not yet**

"Sofi thinks he's in Porpoise Harbor," he reported to Lizzie. "We could get a ride with Jacques. Or . . ." He swallowed. "We could call Mom and Dad."

Lizzie stopped bouncing. "Won't they be mad?"

Leo considered how Mom and Dad would react when they learned that Leo and Lizzie were at a gas station on Porpoise Island alone because Grandpa had been detained by the police.

"Yes," he said with one hundred percent certainty.

She moaned. Then she straightened. "Wait, what about the bees?"

"The bees? Oh right." For a few minutes, he'd entirely forgotten about their mission.

"Shouldn't we keep going?"

"By *ourselves*?"

Lizzie shrugged.

"No way." It was a crazy idea.

"But what if we go to the police and they call Mom and Dad, and Mom and Dad don't let us come back and investigate?" said Lizzie.

She had a point. It was highly unlikely that Mom and Dad would drive them back to Cascadia Farm to search for Grandma's stolen bees. They'd definitely think it was a job for the police.

"What if this is our only chance?"

Leo chewed his lip. They *were* very close to Cascadia Farm . . .

He was still debating when Sawyer came running back. "So do you want a ride?" he asked as Jacques blared the horn again. "Sorry," he added, sounding embarrassed.

Leo tried to weigh the risks involved in continuing on by themselves with the potential benefits. There were almost too many risks to count.

But if they found Grandma's bees, wouldn't it be worth it?

He looked at Lizzie, who mouthed, "Let's keep going!"

"I think we'll stay here," he told Sawyer.

"Yes!" Lizzie cheered.

Sawyer looked concerned. "Are you sure?"

Leo was definitely not sure, but he nodded. "We'll, um, call our mom and dad."

"Well, I guess if you're sure . . ."

"We are," said Lizzie.

"Okay. Bye, then." Sawyer jogged back to the truck and hopped inside. Once again, he'd barely closed the door before Jacques started driving off.

"We're not actually calling Mom and Dad, right?" Lizzie asked once they were gone. "You were lying about that."

"I wasn't exactly lying. We'll call them eventually," said Leo. "After we've investigated the orchard."

She bounced with excitement. "I can't believe we're actually going. By ourselves!"

He couldn't believe it either.

"This is definitely the right thing to do," Lizzie assured him.

"Yeah?" He still wasn't sure.

She nodded. "We have to do it for Grandpa."

"And for Grandma," he added.

"And for adventure!" She punched the air.

He shushed her. Then he quickly texted Sofi to let her know their plans.

This is bananas!! Sofi replied. **KEEP ME POSTED!!!**

It is bananas, he thought as he pocketed his phone. But hopefully, as Lizzie said, it was the right thing to do.

Leo had left his backpack in Grandpa's truck, which meant he didn't have his first aid kit, phone charger, sunscreen or anything else that would help him survive an impromptu adventure. And since Mayhem was occupying Lizzie's backpack, he also had nowhere to store their snacks. So he took off his jacket and stored the snacks inside, then rolled it up and slung it over his shoulder. It would have to do.

He opened the map on his phone and located Cascadia Farm. "It's on Old Orchard Road. I think it'll take us about an hour and a half to get there if we follow the road."

"That's not too far," said Lizzie. "Let's go!" She started to march off, but Leo stopped her.

"Hang on," said Leo. "I think we should try to stay hidden. Two kids walking alone might draw attention." It would in the city, anyway.

"How are we going to do that?"

He studied the map again. He was fairly certain that if they cut across a nearby field, they could stay off the main road *and* reach Cascadia Farm in even less time.

"How would you feel about exercising our right to roam?" he asked Lizzie.

"Oh, I am in," she replied without hesitation.

For once, he was glad to be traveling with an Adventurer.

They left the gas station and started down the road past a blue house with a green barn beside it. They made sure the coast was clear before leaping across the ditch and hurrying into the field beside the barn. Soon they were half-hidden by tall, golden grass that tickled their arms as they walked.

The field turned out to be surprisingly big. After they'd walked for half an hour under the cloudless sky, Lizzie stopped to peel off her jacket and tie it around her waist. They checked on Mayhem in the backpack, ate some jelly beans and continued on.

"You're sure we're going the right way?" Lizzie asked.

Leo showed her the map on his phone. "There's a forest at the other side of the field, see? If we cut through that, we'll reach Old Orchard Road. It shouldn't take too much longer," he added, though it was taking longer than he'd anticipated.

They continued on, ducking under a wooden fence and skirting a herd of cows that paid them no attention.

If Grandpa could see us, Leo thought, he'd be proud.

He hoped that wherever Grandpa was, he was doing okay.

About twenty minutes later, they reached the edge of the forest. Leo checked his map again and confirmed that Old Orchard Road lay just beyond the trees. "It's definitely not far now," he promised, pushing on.

"What'll we do if we find the bees?" asked Lizzie.

Leo hadn't actually considered this. "I guess we'll start by taking photos of the evidence. And then we'll call Mom and Dad. The police too. Or maybe we'll call the police first, since—Hey!" He stopped again. Not twenty feet ahead, where the field met the forest, something was moving in the underbrush. "Do you see that?"

"See what?" Lizzie squinted at the rustling leaves, then gasped. "Is that a kitten?"

It was definitely a small animal—maybe even more than one. "I don't think they're kittens," Leo said. "Maybe rabbits?"

"Leo!" Lizzie squealed as a snout emerged from the bushes, followed by a barrel-shaped body on tiny legs. "They're piglets!" Another piglet followed, then another. Lizzie squealed again. "Oh my gosh, I want one!"

"Hang on," said Leo. The piglets before them did not look like the roly-poly, pink ones he'd raised in *Applewood Acres*. These piglets were darker and faintly striped. These piglets, he realized, were feral. Like the wild pigs that pummeled his pumpkin patch in *Applewood Acres 2: Hog Wild*.

His heart began to race. Not because the piglets themselves were dangerous. But because where there were wild piglets, there were probably wild pig parents.

He was about to warn Lizzie when he heard a noise behind him. It was a grumble-huff. A bit like Grandpa's, but deeper. And angrier.

Leo and Lizzie looked at each other, then slowly turned around.

About fifty feet away stood a big, hairy, dark brown pig. It was roughly the size of a large suitcase, or maybe a shopping cart.

Lizzie sucked in her breath. "Is that . . . ?"

Leo nodded. It had to be.

"Penelope."

CHAPTER 18

Leo knew a thing or two about wild pigs from playing *Applewood Acres 2: Hog Wild.* He knew they could adapt to live in all kinds of habitats and survive brutally cold winters. He knew they were omnivorous and had a varied diet of plants, roots and other animals. He knew they could produce two litters of piglets each year, and since they didn't have many predators, their numbers just kept growing.

But he had no idea what to do when he found himself standing between a wild pig and her piglets.

He decided to run.

He grabbed Lizzie's hand and sprinted for the trees, dodging the piglets, who dove, squealing, into the underbrush. He thought he heard hoofbeats in pursuit, but it could have been his pounding heart, and he didn't want to stop and check.

"Hang on to Mayhem!" he yelled.

"I've got her!" screamed Lizzie.

They sprinted into the forest, which was thankfully less dark and dense than the one on Heron Mountain. There were no boulders to climb over or ferns to push past—just a spongy bed of leaves and needles underfoot. Leo glanced back and saw that Penelope had stopped at the edge of the trees. She was snuffling her piglets.

He slowed to a jog.

"Are we safe?" Lizzie gasped.

"I think so," he said just as Penelope raised her huge, hairy head to stare at them.

Leo felt faint. He reached for the trunk of a nearby tree to steady himself.

Penelope snorted, then started running toward them. Leo had barely opened his mouth to scream when she ground to a halt, less than ten feet away.

"LEO!" Lizzie threw her arms around his waist. "What do we DO?" Inside her backpack, Mayhem mewed.

Leo had no idea. He desperately wished Grandpa were with them. If anyone would know what to do in the face of an angry wild pig, it was Grandpa.

Then suddenly, it came to him. He knew what to do.

"We're going to climb a tree," he told Lizzie.

"We are?" she squeaked.

"Yes." He was almost positive pigs couldn't climb trees.

"Which one?"

"Uh ... this one!" He looked up at the tree he was clutching. There was a limb about a foot above his head that looked sturdy enough to hold them. At least, he thought so—he'd never climbed a tree before so couldn't say for sure.

Penelope took a few steps back and snorted again.

There was no time to lose. Leo crouched and cupped his hands together. "Step here!"

Lizzie put one foot in his hands, and he boosted her up. She scrambled onto the branch, then pulled herself up to a higher one.

Then it was Leo's turn. And he had no one to boost him.

He glanced at Penelope. She returned a cold stare but didn't move.

"Leo, hurry!" cried Lizzie.

He grabbed the branch with both hands and tried to pull himself up. But he wasn't strong enough—he dangled like a kid on the monkey bars, then dropped back down to the ground.

"Use the trunk!" Lizzie yelled.

"What?"

"Like Grandpa did!"

Leo pictured Grandpa scaling the tree that morning. What had he told them? *Brace one foot against a rough area of the trunk. Push into the tree, not down, or your foot will slip.*

He grabbed the branch and tried again, bracing his

right foot against the trunk and pushing hard into the tree. He didn't slip, so he repeated the motion with his left foot, then again with his right. Soon he could reach for a higher branch and pull himself up onto the lowest limb.

"You did it!" Lizzie called from her perch a few feet above his head.

He looked down at the forest floor. Penelope still hadn't moved.

He exhaled shakily. "Are you okay?" he asked Lizzie.

"Uh-huh. Do you think she's going to leave?"

He had no idea. "We'll stay here until she does," he said. "We'll only go back down when we're absolutely, positively sure it's safe. How's Mayhem?"

Lizzie paused. "I think she's asleep."

Leo shook his head. Mayhem and Lizzie were truly meant to be together.

"Good thing we have snacks," said Lizzie. "Can you pass me the jelly beans?"

"Are you kidding!?" A fierce predator was standing right underneath them, and she was thinking about *snacks*?

"I'm hungry!"

"Honestly!" he grumbled. *Very* carefully, he pulled the bag of jelly beans out of his jacket and handed them up to her. "Do *not* move around," he warned. "We are *not* falling out of this tree."

"I don't need to move around to eat." She stuffed some jelly beans into her mouth and chewed noisily.

He rolled his eyes and tried to think. They couldn't stay in the tree forever. Sooner or later Mayhem would get hungry, or one of them would have to pee.

Really, there was only one thing they could do.

"I think it's time to call Mom and Dad," he told Lizzie.

She swallowed her jelly beans. "They'll be so upset."

He nodded. He could only imagine what they'd say when they found out he and Lizzie were stuck in a tree guarded by a feral pig. "But we need help."

"Okay," she sighed.

He pulled out his phone. Sofi had sent five texts since he'd last checked it, but he decided to read them later. He opened his contacts list and was about to tap on Mom's name when Mayhem suddenly let out a howl.

He startled, and the phone slipped through his fingers.

"Nooo!" He tried to grab it, but it was too late. It tumbled to the ground, landing in a pile of leaves.

Lizzie gasped. "Leo!"

"Oh *no*!" he moaned.

Penelope looked at the phone, then up at Leo. She shuffled over to sniff it.

He gasped. "You wouldn't!"

She paused, and then to Leo's absolute horror, she proceeded to pick it up *in her mouth*. She turned and trotted away.

"NO. WAY." He stared after her.

"Did . . . did that really happen?" Lizzie asked.

Leo couldn't believe it. He watched Penelope return to her piglets and herd them off into the field, still carrying his phone.

It was so strange—so completely *bananas*—that he had to laugh. Penelope didn't even glance back.

"Can we go back down now?" asked Lizzie.

"Not yet," he said. "Let's wait until we're sure she's gone. What happened to Mayhem?"

"She wanted to catch a moth, but I wouldn't let her," said Lizzie. "That's why she cried. She's fine now."

Leo leaned against the tree trunk, wishing he could tell Grandpa what had just happened. Or Sofi—she'd freak out when she heard. Then he remembered Sofi's text messages and wondered what they'd said. Now he'd never know.

After what felt like a long time—Leo couldn't tell how long, since he had no clock other than the one on his phone—he decided to risk it. As slowly and quietly as possible, he slid down the trunk. When his feet touched the forest floor, he held his breath, listening for hoofbeats or snorts. But the forest was quiet except for some birds chirping. He signaled for Lizzie to join him.

"Which way do we go?" she asked once she and Mayhem were safely on the ground.

He tried to picture the map on his phone. "That way, I guess." He pointed away from the field they'd crossed. "It shouldn't be too far."

They hurried through the trees, scanning for pigs in pursuit. But Penelope was nowhere to be seen, and before long, they reached the edge of the forest. Beyond it, just as Leo's map had promised, was the road.

He'd never been so happy to see a road.

"We made it!" Lizzie cheered. "We're here!"

"We made it," Leo echoed, feeling dazed. "Well, almost. We still have to get to Cascadia Farm."

"Pfft. Easy!" said Lizzie. "It's just a short walk, right?"

He nodded. A short walk down a road was nothing compared to what they'd just done: exercising their right to roam, outwitting a notorious wild pig, navigating an unfamiliar forest. Most islanders probably hadn't even done all those things.

Grandpa would definitely be proud of them, Leo decided, drawing himself up tall. "All we have to do is follow Old Orchard Road," he said. It sounded so simple.

"You mean South Point Road," said Lizzie.

"Huh? No, it's definitely Old Orchard."

"But what about that?" She pointed to a sign on the opposite side of the road.

"South Point Road," he read aloud. "Wait, that's not right!"

"Uh-oh," said Lizzie. "Do you know where South Point Road goes?"

He tried to picture his map, but couldn't recall seeing a South Point Road anywhere on it. "You've got to be kidding," he groaned. They'd come so far, only to find themselves on the wrong road!

As he fretted about what to do next, a car appeared on the road, headed toward them. If the driver thought it strange to see two kids out by themselves, they didn't show it. The car blew right past, blaring music through its open windows. It zipped up the hill to their right, turned a corner and disappeared.

"Maybe they're going to Cascadia Farm," Lizzie said wistfully. "Think they'd give us a ride?"

Leo shook his head and tried to think. Surely if he could outwit Penelope, he could think of a solution for this new problem.

Lizzie nudged him. "Grandpa said that's how the islanders get around, remember? People with extra space in their cars help people who need a lift. And we could really use a lift."

"Hitchhike?" He turned to her in disbelief. "No way. That's a crazy idea!"

She shrugged. "It's how the islanders get around. We're basically islanders now, aren't we?"

He opened his mouth, then shut it. They *had* just exercised their right to roam, outwitted a notorious wild pig and navigated an unfamiliar forest. They'd also eaten seaweed and chanterelle mushrooms and watched orcas from the ferry deck. They'd even climbed a mountain and gazed out on the great Pacific Ocean.

Maybe Lizzie was right and they *were* basically island-ers now. Maybe like Grandma and Grandpa, they were a part of the islands, and the islands were a part of them.

He took a deep breath. "Okay. We'll do it."

"*We will*?" She looked shocked.

He nodded. "It's what the islanders do, right?"

She blinked at him, then nodded vigorously. "Yes! Let's do it!"

They walked to the edge of the road and looked both ways. To their left, the road went downhill. To the right, it climbed up. "Let's go right," Leo decided. "Maybe at the top of the hill we'll be able to see Cascadia Farm."

Lizzie agreed. "So how do we hitchhike?"

He pictured the teenagers on Heron Island. "We stick our thumbs out, like this." He demonstrated, and Lizzie did the same.

They walked up the hill, thumbs held high, and a breeze picked up, carrying the now-familiar smells of the forest and the sea. Leo breathed it in, feeling his lungs expand.

It was a long hill, but nothing like the climb up Heron Mountain. When they reached the top, they stopped and turned to look back. And just as Leo had hoped, they could suddenly see for miles. There were deep green forests and fawn-colored fields and farmhouses connected by little winding roads. And beyond all that lay the great Pacific Ocean, dark blue and sparkling in the sun.

Leo took it all in, and the feeling he'd had on the peak of Heron Mountain came back to him again. He was once again bold and capable.

And yes, even adventurous.

He squared his shoulders and shaded his eyes from the sun. And it occurred to him, as he looked out over the forests and farms of Porpoise Island, that there were so many directions they could take—so many places to explore. They could head down to the beach or pick a mountain to climb. They could spend the night outside and sleep under the stars. The options suddenly seemed endless.

And maybe . . . maybe the same went for him. Maybe Mo was right, and he wasn't actually destined to spend his life at a desk checking people's taxes. Maybe he could be something else, like a detective. Or a doctor. Or a beekeeper.

The possibilities began to pile up like questions in his brain. He could be a farmer. A tree topper. A ferry captain. A veterinarian. A search and rescue paramedic. A postal delivery person. An astronaut. A chef in a Michelin-starred restaurant.

The options were infinite. The world was enormous. Leo felt dizzy, in the very best way.

"A car!" Lizzie shouted as a little, blue car passed them, then slowed. "Leo, it's stopping!"

He shook himself back to the present. "It is?" He gasped. "It is!"

"We did it!" She cheered. "We got a ride!"

They ran toward the car, which had stopped on the side of the road.

"We're coming!" Leo hollered. "We're—"

The driver's door opened, and Dad leaped out, his eyes wide with horror.

They screeched to a halt.

"Uh-oh," whispered Lizzie.

"Dead," Leo finished. "We're dead."

CHAPTER 19

"Your right to *roam*?" Dad repeated. "Your RIGHT to ROAM?!"

"Alex, calm down," said Mom.

"What even *is* a right to roam?" He threw his hands in the air, inadvertently smacking the car's rearview mirror.

"Well, in countries like Norway and Scotland," Lizzie began, "people can roam anywhere they want—"

"Lizzie," Leo hissed. This was definitely not the time.

Dad stared at them for a long moment, then turned to Mom. "I just can't believe this!"

They were still parked on the side of South Point Road, but now Leo and Lizzie were in the back seat of the rental car, with Lizzie's backpack and Leo's jacket full of snacks at their feet. Mom and Dad had yet to notice the kitten napping inside Lizzie's backpack, and Lizzie had yet to mention her. For the past twenty minutes, she and Leo had been trying to explain why Mom and Dad had found them hitchhiking on Porpoise Island. Mom and Dad, who'd been on their way to a cheese-tasting tour at the farmers' market, seemed far more concerned about the risks Leo and Lizzie had taken than all the brave and capable things they'd done. And they hadn't even told them about escaping Penelope yet!

"Okay. Let's pause for a second." Mom took a deep breath. "The most important thing is that everyone is safe."

"Except Grandpa!" cried Lizzie. "We don't even know where he is!"

"And Grandma's bees," Leo added.

"Right," said Mom. "But we're going to go find Grandpa right away. I just..." She sighed. "I don't understand why you didn't tell us you were here on the island."

"We knew you'd worry," said Lizzie.

"Well, of course we'd worry!" Dad exclaimed.

Mom put a hand on his arm. "We'll talk more about this later. Right now, let's go back to Porpoise Harbor and find Grandpa."

"I can't believe Sam got himself arrested," Dad grumbled as he started the car.

"Maybe not arrested," Leo piped up. "We don't know that for sure."

At that point, Mayhem woke up. She poked her head out of Lizzie's backpack and let out a small but distinct mew. Lizzie coughed to cover it up, but not before Dad heard.

He shut the car engine off. "What was that?"

"Um . . ." Lizzie looked at Leo.

"Is that a cat?" Dad turned to look at them. "Do you have a CAT in your backpack?"

"Not exactly." Lizzie pulled Mayhem out to show him. "She's still a kitten, see? Her name is Mayhem."

Dad recoiled, as if Lizzie had just pulled out a python.

"Lizzie!" Mom cried.

"Please let me keep her!" Lizzie begged. "Mayhem and I are meant to be together. Right, Leo?"

"They really are," he agreed.

Dad groaned, then sneezed.

"Okay. Let's go back to the resort," said Mom. "I'll go to the police station and find Grandpa. Then we'll figure out what to do next."

"So I can keep Mayhem?" asked Lizzie.

"No!" said Dad.

"We'll talk about it later, Lizzie," said Mom.

Dad had just pulled back onto the road when Leo suddenly remembered the most important thing: their mission. "Wait!" he cried. "What about the bees? Can't we go investigate?"

"*We* are not investigating," Dad told him. "That's a job for the police."

"But—"

"No buts, Leo!"

Leo grumble-huffed. Lizzie did too.

When they reached the Porpoise Island Spa and Resort, Mom climbed into the driver's seat, promising to return soon with Grandpa.

"Can't we come with you?" asked Leo.

She shook her head. "You stay here. Maybe take a shower—you've got sap in your hair. How did that happen?"

He thought about the time he'd spent sitting on a tree branch, legs dangling over a wild pig. "It's a bit of a long story."

She sighed. "Later then."

"But the cat can't come in," Dad pointed out.

"Her name is *Mayhem*!" Lizzie declared. "And if she's not coming in, I'm not either."

Mom rubbed her temples. "Alex, ask the concierge if the cat can come inside for a while. I bet she'll make an exception if you explain the situation."

Dad doubted it, but he went to ask. Minutes later, he returned. "She said it's okay, but only for a few hours. The cat . . . *Mayhem* . . . can't stay overnight."

Lizzie shrugged as she followed him inside. "We don't want to stay overnight anyway."

The Porpoise Island Spa and Resort was perched on a cliff overlooking the ocean. It was sprawling and spotless, with sparkling chandeliers and classical music playing softly in every room. Leo could see why Mom and Dad liked it so much—and why Grandpa would hate it.

They spent a few miserable hours in Mom and Dad's room staring out the window at the ocean and waiting for Mom to return. When she did, she looked exhausted. She collapsed on the bed and told them what had happened.

Grandpa had been on his way back to the gas station when the police pulled him over for driving too fast. Porpoise Island, it turned out, *did* have a speed limit, and Grandpa had broken it. Before long, however, the police noticed that Grandpa's insurance had expired *and* he had a lot of unpaid parking tickets. Fifteen years of unpaid parking tickets, to be exact.

An argument had ensued, and words were exchanged—rude words, according to Mom, but she wouldn't say which ones. Then the police had taken Grandpa to the station, where he'd had to pay off his tickets and renew his insurance.

"Béatriz was at the station when I got there," Mom added. "Her daughter Sofi too."

"They were?" Leo exclaimed. "Why?"

She turned over and propped her head on a big pillow. "When Sofi texted you but didn't hear back, she got worried and told her mom what she knew. Why didn't you text her back, Leo?"

He recalled Penelope trotting away with his phone. He wasn't sure Mom could handle that story. "I, um, lost my phone."

"You lost your phone!" Dad exclaimed. "How?"

"I dropped it in the forest." He gave Lizzie a meaning-ful look, and she nodded.

Dad sighed. "This is all just so unlike you, Leo."

"Where's Grandpa now?" he asked, eager to change the subject.

"Outside in his truck," Mom said. "We drove to the gas station so he could pick it up. I told him he could stay here with us tonight, since the last ferry to Heron Island already left. I even offered to pay for his own room. But he refused. He says he's going to stay with Mo." She sighed. "We'll all take the ferry back to Heron Island tomorrow morning."

"I'll go to Mo's too!" cried Lizzie.

"Me too," Leo added, picturing them all sitting around the fire, sipping huckleberry soda and listening to Grandpa and Mo laugh about old times. "Can we, Mom? Please?"

"No," she said firmly. "You're both staying here. And I'm sorry, Lizzie, but the cat . . ."

"Mayhem!" said Lizzie.

"*Mayhem* has to go with Grandpa."

Lizzie began to cry. Mom looked pained.

Leo knew it was no use. "Come on," he whispered to Lizzie. "It's just for one night. She'll be okay."

"But *I* won't!" Lizzie wailed, hugging Mayhem to her chest.

He put an arm around her shoulders and steered her toward the door.

They found Grandpa sitting in his truck in the parking lot, his hat pulled down over his eyes and his mouth puckered.

"Grandpa!" Lizzie banged on the window, startling him. "We want to come to Mo's!"

Grandpa rolled down the window and pushed his hat up. "Looks like I got us all in trouble," he said.

"It's okay," said Leo. "We're sorry we didn't make it to Cascadia Farm. We were really, really close!"

Grandpa sighed. "It wouldn't have mattered. The bees aren't there."

"What do you mean?"

Grandpa explained that when he'd reached the police station, he'd called Mo straight away. She'd sent Corny to the gas station to look for Leo and Lizzie, and when he couldn't find them, he drove on to Cascadia Farm. He would have been there to meet them had Mom and Dad not found them first.

"While he was there, he had a look around and talked to the orchardists," Grandpa told them. "They told them they'd ended up borrowing hives from another local beekeeper. Corny called her just to make sure. They don't have Evelyn's bees."

Leo's shoulders slumped. The day just got worse and worse.

"I'm heading back to Mo's now. And I hear I'm taking Mayhem?" Grandpa looked at Lizzie.

She sniffled. "Will you take such good care of her?"

Promising he would, Grandpa got out of the truck and took Mayhem from Lizzie's arms, then put her in the crate on the floor. When he closed the crate door, Mayhem let out a sad mew. They all winced.

Then Grandpa got back in the truck and drove away.

CHAPTER 20

The next morning, Leo was slouched in the back seat of the rental car, staring out at the parking lot of the Porpoise Island Spa and Resort, where they'd all spent the night. He and Lizzie were showered and scrubbed, and their clothes were spotless again thanks to the resort's laundry services. They'd eaten well at the restaurant and slept on clean sheets.

And they were completely, utterly miserable.

They were also grounded in perpetuity.

"That means forever," Leo had told Lizzie when Mom and Dad broke the news.

"I figured," she'd grunted.

"Everyone buckled in?" Dad looked at them through the rearview mirror. "We don't move until you are."

Lizzie replied with a grumble-huff.

"We're buckled in," Leo told him.

"Let's go, Alex," said Mom. "We don't want to miss the ferry."

"Grandpa will definitely be on it, right?" Lizzie said. "With Mayhem?"

"When I called him last night, he said he'd be there," Mom told her.

"With Mayhem?"

"With Mayhem."

"Dad, can you drive a little faster?" Lizzie asked.

"Absolutely not," Dad replied.

She didn't say another word as they drove—excessively slowly, Leo had to agree—to the ferry terminal.

Once they'd boarded and parked on the lower deck, Mom suggested they all go up to the café for an early lunch. "If I remember correctly, they make great grilled cheese sandwiches," she said.

"Can Grandpa come?" asked Lizzie.

"Of course," said Mom. "Go ask him."

Leo and Lizzie hopped out of the car and dashed to the truck, which was parked two rows over. Grandpa rolled down his window when he saw them.

"Want to come to the café for grilled cheese?" Leo asked at the same time Lizzie demanded to know if Mayhem was okay.

"No," Grandpa said to Leo. "And yes," he told Lizzie. "She's asleep in her crate. But you can't bring her up on deck this time."

Lizzie pouted.

190

"Hey, Grandpa," said Leo. "I've been thinking about the bees and where we should investigate next." He'd had a lot of time to consider this the previous evening, since there was very little for a kid to do at the Porpoise Island Spa and Resort. Especially a kid whose cell phone had been stolen by a wild pig.

But before he could share his ideas, Grandpa shook his head. "It's over."

"What's over?"

"The search for the bees," he said. "I'm giving up. They're as good as gone."

"Gone!" Leo couldn't believe it. "But we don't know that! We haven't even—"

"Leo! Lizzie!" called Dad. "Come on, let's go."

"Coming!" Leo shouted, then turned back to Grandpa, who'd begun to roll up his window.

"Let's talk about this when we get home." Grandpa closed the window and pulled his hat down over his eyes. Leo stared at him for a moment, then turned to go. It hurt too much to stay.

They tromped upstairs to the café, where Mom ordered grilled cheese sandwiches and found a table near the window looking out to sea. The sky was a brilliant, cloudless blue, which didn't suit Leo's mood at all.

"Look, there's Béatriz and Sofi!" Mom pointed. They were sitting at a table on the opposite side of the café, laughing at something on Sofi's phone. "Do you want to go say hi, Leo?"

He shook his head.

"There's Jin. And is that Marguerite?" Mom waved. "Wow, I guess everyone spent the weekend on Porpoise Island!"

Leo turned to see the Bumblers at another table, sipping milkshakes.

"I'm going to say hello. Leo and Lizzie, do you want to come?"

"Nope," said Lizzie, her mouth full of grilled cheese. Leo declined too. There was only one person he cared to talk to, and that person was in a truck on the lower deck of the ferry.

"Can I go to the bathroom?" he asked.

"Sure," said Dad. "Can you find it by yourself?"

"Definitely." Leo hopped up and hurried out of the café. He headed for the bathroom, but when he reached it, he continued on toward the stairs that would take him to the lower deck. He'd almost reached them when someone called his name.

"Leo, wait up!" Sofi came running after him. "I've been dying to talk to you. I texted you a million times yesterday, but you didn't answer!" She stopped beside him at the top of the stairs. "What happened?"

"It's kind of a long story," he told her. "But I don't have much time right now. I have to go find Grandpa."

"I'll come," she said. "And you can tell me your story. A short version, at least."

They started down the stairs, and Leo tried to tell a short version of the story, starting with the part he knew she'd care about the most.

"She stole your PHONE!?" Sofi yelled, startling a family climbing up the stairs. "SERIOUSLY?"

"Seriously," said Leo.

"That's incredible!" she marveled. "It's just like *Applewood Acres 2: Hog Wild*. Except, like, real life!"

"Exactly." He was glad she understood.

"And you know what this means, right?" she went on. "There isn't just one Penelope on Porpoise Island!"

"Huh?"

"If she has piglets, there has to be another wild pig. Maybe a . . . Peter." Sofi grinned.

This hadn't even occurred to Leo, but of course she was right. He went on to tell her about Mo's cozy house in the woods and the delicious meal Corny had made and how Grandpa had climbed a tree to rescue Mayhem.

"I can't believe I thought Mo was a man," Sofi said as they wove between cars on the lower deck. "She sounds pretty cool. I feel bad for calling her a criminal."

"She's really great," Leo agreed, scanning the deck for Grandpa's truck.

"Well, next time someone mentions that rumor, I'm going to squash it," she said decidedly. "Oh, hey, it's Sawyer!"

He was sitting on the tailgate of Jacques's truck, whittling a piece of wood with a Swiss Army knife. When he saw them, he leaped off and ran over. "Is your Grandpa okay, Leo? What happened?"

"He's fine," Leo said, wishing he'd noted where Grandpa had parked. "He's down here somewhere. . ."

Sawyer turned to Sofi. "Why didn't you come yesterday?"

"I was at the police station," she said, sounding rather pleased.

"You *were*?"

"Wait, you missed the birthday party?" Leo asked. "I didn't know that."

"Yep." She didn't look at all upset. "How was it?"

"Not bad," said Sawyer. "The cake was double-chocolate."

Leo stopped listening and resumed his search for Grandpa's truck. Finally, he spotted it, three rows away. "I have to go," he told them, and he was about to run off when he noticed the wood in Sawyer's hand. "Wait, what's that?"

"This? Just a piece I found in the truck." Sawyer gestured at a pile of wood and tools in the truck bed. "It's nothing special—not yet, anyway. I want to smooth out this broken edge." He held it out, and Leo took it.

Sawyer was right—there was nothing special about this piece of wood. It was old and worn, about the size of a tablet. But it felt oddly familiar. Leo turned it over and found two words stamped onto the wood, near the jagged edge. "NICE DAY!"

Sawyer shrugged. "I don't know what that's about, but I kind of like it."

Leo was about to hand it back when all of a sudden, he knew what it was about. Or at least he thought he might. "Hey, can I borrow this?" he asked.

Sawyer looked surprised. "Um, sure. You can keep it if you want."

"Thanks," Leo said. "I have to go." He hurried off toward Grandpa's truck.

"Leo, wait!" Sofi jogged after him. "What's going on? You're acting weird."

"I have to get Grandpa," he told her. "And then Lizzie. Come on!"

Ten minutes later, they burst into the café, winded from sprinting up the stairs. A crowd had gathered at Mom and Dad's table: Béatriz, Jin and Marguerite were all there, eating grilled cheese sandwiches and chatting loudly. Despite all the noise, Lizzie was fast asleep on Mom's lap.

When Mom saw Grandpa, she did a double take. "Dad?"

"Leo, where have you been?" asked Dad. "I was getting worried."

"We went down to the car deck—" he began.

"The car deck!" cried Dad. "You said you were going to the bathroom!"

Before Leo could explain, Bruno appeared beside them, dressed in a navy blue ferry worker's uniform. "Sam, I need to have a word with you!"

Grandpa waved him off. "Not now, Bruno."

Bruno put his fists on his hips. "I know what you did the other night!"

"Wait, Bruno." Marguerite held up a hand. "I think something's wrong."

"I'll tell you what's wrong—"

"Not *now*!" Grandpa snapped.

"Can you all just listen?" Leo pleaded, but his voice was lost in the clamor.

"Dad, do you want a grilled cheese?" Mom asked Grandpa.

"Mom, you'll never guess what we found!" Sofi said to Béatriz.

"Leo, I'm concerned about your behavior," Dad fretted.

Leo took a deep breath, then hollered, "EVERYONE LISTEN!"

The whole café fell silent.

Finally, Lizzie woke up. "What's going on?" She yawned.

Leo turned to her. "Where's the scratch pad?"

"The what?"

"Mayhem's scratch pad. You still have it, right?"

"Oh yeah." She picked her backpack up off the floor and pulled it out.

Grandpa took it from her, and Leo held up the piece of wood he'd borrowed from Sawyer. Their jagged edges fit together perfectly.

They turned the pieces over so they could read the words together.

HIVE A NICE DAY!

"It's a pun," Leo whispered.

"A pretty bad pun," Lizzie observed.

"A perfect pun." Grandpa smiled.

Mom stared at the wood. "Is that . . . ?"

"We think so," said Leo. "Right, Grandpa?"

Grandpa nodded. "Evelyn's beekeeper stamp. I didn't even know she had one. But of course she did." He traced the words with his finger.

"So what does this mean?" Mom asked.

Leo looked at Grandpa. "It means that when we get to Heron Island, we need to go for a hike."

"A hike?" Mom looked alarmed.

"A hike?" Dad grimaced.

"A hike," Sofi confirmed.

"Sounds like an adventure!" Lizzie hopped off Mom's lap. "Can I bring Mayhem? She won't want to miss this."

CHAPTER 21

"I can't believe we're doing this," Dad muttered as he climbed over a moss-covered log.

"We're almost there," Leo assured him as he hurried to keep up with Grandpa, who was leading the way up Heron Mountain. Lizzie was close behind him, with Mayhem in her backpack. Then came Dad and Mom, Sofi and Béatriz. Jin, Marguerite and Bruno brought up the rear. Once the Bumblers had heard Leo's theory about the missing bees, they'd all insisted on coming along. Grandpa had protested, but they wouldn't be deterred.

"There's strength in numbers, Sam," Marguerite had told him. "If Jacques is indeed the thief, he'll have to answer to us all!"

"I never liked that guy!" Bruno added. He'd ended his shift early so he could join the investigation too.

Just before the ferry docked, Jin found Jacques and paid him to pick up twenty pounds of flour at the grocery store and deliver it to the Driftwood Café. That way, he'd be nowhere near his property when they arrived to search.

And it's a good thing, Leo thought as they crashed through the forest, because we're the most conspicuous bunch of detectives ever. At one point, Marguerite and Bruno even began to sing a marching song that involved a lot of buzzing, but Grandpa ordered them to cut it out.

"I don't understand why we couldn't stick to the trail," Mom said as she hopped over a mud puddle.

"It's a shortcut," Lizzie told her. "Sort of."

"And we need to look for more evidence," Leo added. He kept his eyes on the forest floor, scanning for signs of the missing bees.

"We should also be looking for ticks," Dad piped up. "The concierge at the resort told me that they're particularly bad on Heron Island."

"Oh, they are," Béatriz agreed. "I've removed ticks from *hundreds* of patients over the years."

This prompted everyone to start sharing their own stories about ticks. Leo was very close to ordering them to *cut it out* so he could concentrate when Grandpa stopped suddenly. Leo looked up and saw him standing underneath the Private Property sign. "This is it!" he cried.

Grandpa squinted up at the sign and shook his head. "I still don't understand where he could have hidden the bees. I searched his property two days ago."

"We'll all go with you this time," said Jin. "Eight pairs of eyes are better than one."

Grandpa didn't look convinced, but he started off toward Jacques's house.

"Wait, isn't this trespassing?" Dad pointed up at the sign. "That's not allowed."

Bruno tsked. "Haven't you ever heard of your right to roam?"

"That is *not* a real thing," said Dad.

"It absolutely is!" Bruno insisted, and he began to explain how things worked in Norway and Scotland. Leo hurried off after Grandpa.

They emerged from the forest just below Jacques's house, which was perched on the rocks overlooking the ocean. What little yard he had was rocky and uneven. Like Grandpa had said, there weren't many places to hide a dozen beehives.

Still, they all fanned out and searched the property, clambering over boulders and peering behind trees. But no one found a single bee, let alone a dozen hives.

"Maybe we need to regroup," Jin suggested once they'd conducted a thorough search. "Why don't we go to the café? I don't know about you, but I find tea and cinnamon buns help me think."

"I know!" Marguerite snapped her fingers. "Let's drop in on Willa. She lives right next door to Jacques and always has cookies on hand."

"She makes wonderful lemon shortbread," said Bruno.

"Snickerdoodles too," Jin added. They headed back the way they'd come.

"Willa?" Leo murmured. He hadn't thought about the fourth Bumbler since he'd seen her at the Driftwood Café. He turned to Sofi. "Willa lives next door?"

She nodded, then began to follow the others.

Leo hung back and did a quick brainstorm, a technique he'd learned from Peregrine Peabody. It involved calling to mind everything you knew about a person or place or thing.

Unfortunately, he knew nothing about Willa, except that she had a showercap and a healthy fear of Grandpa.

Sofi turned back. "Coming?"

He sighed and started after her, then stopped suddenly as a memory came to mind.

He *did* know something about Willa.

"Hey Sofi," he called. "How do you get to be the president of the Bumblers?"

She raised an eyebrow over her bright-blue glasses. "Whoever wins the most prizes at the Heron Island Honey Festival is named president for the year. Ideally they'd win Honey of the Year—that's the best prize."

"Honey of the Year," Leo repeated.

"It's really not the best system," Sofi went on. "I mean, just because your bees make good honey doesn't mean you're cut out for a leadership role—"

But Leo had stopped listening and was running off, shouting for Grandpa.

Marguerite was not convinced. Willa, she insisted, was an upstanding member of the Heron Island community. She was *not* a bee thief.

Still, she agreed to knock on Willa's door and provide a distraction while the others quickly searched her yard. Leo led the way back to the Private Property sign, then turned left, toward the other house he'd seen when looking down from the peak of Heron Mountain. Marguerite headed for Willa's front door, and the others veered off toward the small yard below her house.

They'd only just stepped out of the forest when Grandpa let out a shout. He pushed past Leo and ran into the clearing.

"The hives!" Leo yelled when he saw them stacked on some big, flat rocks with a view of the forest and the ocean beyond. There were six blue boxes—Willa's own bees, Leo guessed—and eleven white ones that looked very much like Grandma's.

Béatriz blazed past him, hot on Grandpa's heels. Leo could hear her warning Grandpa to be careful and not get too close, and Grandpa retorting that he'd get as close as he pleased, thank you very much.

Moments later, Béatriz hollered, "HIVE A NICE DAY! These are Evelyn's bees!"

"Yes!" Sofi threw her arms in the air.

"We did it!" Lizzie started dancing. Mayhem yowled from the backpack.

And over near the hives, Grandpa sank quietly to his knees.

Mom hurried to join him. She knelt on the rocky ground and put an arm around his shoulders.

"Leo, we did it!" Lizzie twirled around him. "We found the bees! I mean, mostly you found them. But Mayhem and I helped."

"We did it," he agreed, feeling like he too might need to sit down.

Dad joined them, looking stunned. "Wow, Leo. That was impressive! But . . . how did you know the bees were here?"

Leo took a deep breath, feeling a bit like Peregrine Peabody, who at the end of every game explained how he'd cracked the case. "I only knew one thing about Willa," he began. "She wanted to be the next president of the Heron Island Bumblers. She said so the day the bees went missing, but I forgot about it until just now. And to become president, you have to win the most prizes at the Heron Island Honey Festival. Ideally Honey of the Year."

"Honey of the Year?"

He nodded. "Grandma won it a bunch of times. She made the best honey on all the islands."

He looked over at Grandpa, who was still on the ground, leaning into Mom.

"So I thought maybe that was her motive," he finished. "If she had prize-winning bees, she could finally be president."

"Wow." Dad rubbed his forehead. "That's . . ."

"Bananas," Leo finished.

"Totally."

"I know."

Dad smiled. "You know, Leo, I'm starting to wonder if you're actually more of a Problem Solver."

"No way, Dad," said Lizzie. "Leo's an Adventurer."

Leo grinned. "The thing is, I don't think I'm any one of those things—a Problem Solver or an Auditor or an Adventurer. Not entirely, anyway. I . . . I'm just me."

Dad was quiet for a moment. Finally, he nodded. "I think you're right, Leo. And in any case, you should be really proud of yourself."

Leo smiled. He was.

Lizzie slipped her hand into his, and Dad put his arms around them both. They stood like that for a long time, while the Bumblers inspected the hives and Mom and Grandpa sat quietly on the rocks and the bees swirled above them in the brilliant blue sky above the ocean that seemed to stretch on forever.

CHAPTER 22

"You could definitely teach Mayhem to sit on command," Lizzie told Sofi. "And shake a paw too—that's pretty easy. If I were staying, I'd teach her to ride a skateboard."

Sofi looked skeptical. "You can teach a cat to ride a skateboard?"

"You need to watch Pandora Ali's videos," said Lizzie. "How often are you going to visit Mayhem again?"

"She told you three times already," Leo groaned.

It was their second-last day on Heron Island, and they were sitting with Sofi on the steps of Grandpa's back porch, watching Mayhem prowl for mice in the grass.

"I'll come at least once a week," Sofi promised again.

Lizzie nodded. "And can we do video calls? That way I can talk to Mayhem so she won't forget me."

"Sure," said Sofi. "But she's not going to forget you."

Lizzie sighed. "I hope not."

Leo had expected Lizzie to put up a big fight when Mom and Dad sat her down and told her she couldn't bring Mayhem back to Toronto—it just wasn't possible with Dad's allergies. But she'd shown remarkable composure, mostly thanks to Grandpa, who'd stepped in and promised to care for Mayhem himself. She was family now, he'd said. His home was Mayhem's home.

"Sawyer said he'd come too," said Sofi. "He has more time now that he isn't working for Jacques."

"Is he doing okay?" asked Leo. He hadn't seen Sawyer since the day they'd met on the ferry and Sawyer had handed him the evidence of Grandma's missing bees. That was only two days ago, but so much had happened since!

After finding Grandma's bees in Willa's yard, they'd called the police right away. It had taken them a while to get there, but there was no danger of Willa escaping. According to Marguerite, she was too embarrassed to leave her house—and probably too scared to face Grandpa. When the police eventually arrived, she let them inside, offered them lemon shortbread (they declined) and confessed that she'd stolen Grandma's bees in the hopes of taking home top prize at the Heron Island Honey Festival.

But that wasn't all. Willa also revealed that she hadn't done it alone. She'd paid her neighbor Jacques to drive to Grandpa's late at night, haul the beehives away in his truck and set them up in her yard.

Apparently, Grandpa was right: you really could pay Jacques of All Trades to do almost anything.

Sawyer had been stunned by the news. He hadn't suspected a thing.

"I texted him yesterday," Sofi told Leo. "He's doing okay. He definitely won't miss working for Jacques. And now that he has more time, he's going to look into joining Whittle by Whittle."

"Joining what?"

"That's the Heron Island woodworking guild," she explained.

Leo snorted. "Did Grandma name it?"

Sofi grinned. "How did you know?"

"Maybe Sawyer can make Mayhem a cat condo!" said Lizzie. "Pandora Ali sells them on her website. I asked Grandpa if he'd buy her one, but he said no cat of his would be living in a condo."

Leo and Sofi laughed.

Grandpa had also shown remarkable composure since they'd found the missing bees. He hadn't spewed curse words or stomped on his hat when the police came to his house later that day and confirmed what Willa had done. He even managed to keep his cool when he'd learned that Jacques, who had no experience moving bees, had dropped a hive while unloading it and damaged the box and the colony inside. He'd tossed the broken box into the woods near his house, where Leo and Lizzie (or rather, Mayhem) had found it.

The Bumblers were incensed when they heard. They'd descended on Grandpa's house that evening for an impromptu meeting in his kitchen.

"Rule Number One of beekeeping," Marguerite had declared, thumping the table with her fist, "is that you never harm your bees or anyone else's. And that's exactly what Willa did. All because she wanted to be president!" She shook her head. "I still can't believe it."

"It's *bee*-fuddling," said Jin.

"*Bee*-wildering," Bruno added from his perch on the counter.

It was a shame, Grandpa agreed. And according to the police, both criminals could face time in prison. "But frankly," he said as he passed around mugs of hot tea, "I don't really care about that. All I want is to bring the bees home and make sure they're healthy. *That's* my new mission."

If that weren't surprising enough, he then turned to the Bumblers and asked if they'd help him.

"I have a very good book." He patted the cover of *Everything Bees.* "But people can be helpful too. Some of them, anyway."

Marguerite and Jin's mouths fell wide open. Bruno nearly tumbled off the counter. Once they'd recovered, they told Grandpa that they'd be happy to help. Delighted, even.

Late that night, after everyone had gone home, Leo found Grandpa drawing up plans for a big garden he wanted to plant beside the beehives, to help them with their pollen collection. He also planned to fix the drooping fences and get rid of the rusty old equipment lying around the farm.

He looked like he had when he was climbing down the tree at Mo's place: as if a light had been lit deep inside him.

Finding the bees had given him a new sense of purpose—he'd actually said that to the reporter for the *Heron Herald*, who'd come to interview him, Leo and Lizzie the next day. She'd assured them it would make the front page, since it was the biggest news the island had seen.

"The biggest buzz," Lizzie had corrected her. "You can use that."

The reporter thanked her and said she just might.

They had yet to see the story since the *Heron Herald* only came out twice a week. But Grandpa was certain it would be published the next morning—their last morning on Heron Island. They planned to pick up several copies on their way to the ferry.

"I can't believe you're leaving so soon!" Sofi lamented. "We didn't even get to play *Applewood Acres 4: Shenanigoats!*"

"We can play together online," Leo told her. "But I know, it's not the same. I wish we could stay." He certainly never thought he'd hear himself say that.

"Forever!" Lizzie scooped Mayhem up from the grass and planted a kiss on her nose.

Leo wasn't sure about forever. But he did wish they lived closer. Still, he had a feeling they'd be back before long, maybe even as soon as the winter break. He'd asked Mom and Dad about it, and they hadn't said no, which was promising.

Lizzie thought the two of them ought to return alone, but Leo doubted Mom and Dad would agree to that—Dad was still talking about the hitchhiking incident and probably would be for a long time. But maybe Mom and Dad would drop them off at Grandpa's, then go to the Porpoise Island Spa and Resort again. Mom would probably like that.

Just that morning, she and Leo had taken a special trip by themselves to see the memorial mural at the Driftwood Café. They'd invited Grandpa and Lizzie along, but Lizzie wanted to spend the entire day with Mayhem, and Grandpa said he'd go by himself another time.

Mom cried a little when she read the sticky notes, and they took selfies in front of the mural. Then they ate cinnamon buns outside among the wildflowers, and Mom told Leo about the adventures Grandma took her on when she was a kid, most of which resulted in her getting very dirty and sometimes soaking wet.

"I didn't love those adventures," she admitted. "But I'm glad for them now because I can remember her doing what she loved best in the place she loved the most." She stayed quiet for a moment, then smiled. "Sounds like a pretty good way to live your life, doesn't it?"

Leo agreed. He thought of it now as he sat in the sun on Grandpa's porch steps. Maybe someday he too would be doing what he loved best in the place he loved most. He had no idea what or where that would be, but that was okay. In fact, it was rather exciting.

"So I was doing some research last night," said Sofi. "And I found an article about beekeepers in Toronto who keep their bees on rooftops. You should look into that when you get home," she advised. "Rooftop beekeeping would be so cool."

Leo pictured himself on a rooftop in Toronto, dressed in a beekeeping suit, looking out on the city from way up high just as he'd looked out on the islands and the ocean from the top of Heron Mountain. Even a week ago, it would have seemed unfathomable. But now . . .

"I'll look into it," he told her. "You never know."

ACKNOWLEDGMENTS

As always, I have so many people to thank for working with me on *The Big Sting* and helping get it out into the world.

First and foremost, to Lynne Missen for the thought and care she puts into every single book and for generally being a wonderful person.

To the marketing and publicity team at Tundra Books, who work tirelessly to promote books for young readers and deserve all the praise.

To Yvette Ghione for her sharp copyedit and Catherine Marjoribanks for proofreading, and to Bharti Bedi, production editor extraordinaire.

To Morgan Goble for the amazing cover illustration and to Emma Dolan for designing a beautiful book.

To the Inkslingers—Stacey Matson, Tanya Kyi, Holman Wang, Kallie George, Kay Weisman, Lori Sherritt and Sara Gillingham—who gave excellent feedback early on.

And to Eric Simons, who read early drafts, helped me work through the stickiest problems and listened to me drone on about hive heists for years (puns very much intended).

To my beekeeping pal Jode Roberts for answering many, many questions about bees and how one might steal them (not that he has).

To my agent Amy Tompkins for all her support.

And last but certainly not least, a huge thank you to the Canada Council for the Arts for supporting this novel and allowing Canadian creators to keep on creating.

Finally, a note about hive heists. While the one in this story is fictional, bee theft is not uncommon thanks to declining pollinator populations around the world. I learned a lot about hive heists from stories in the Guardian, CBC, National Geographic and NPR. If you're interested, you can find more information and links on my website: rachelledelaney.com.

RACHELLE DELANEY is the author of nine novels for young readers, including *Alice Fleck's Recipes for Disaster*, which was an Ontario Library Association Silver Birch Honour Book and was shortlisted for several other awards, including the Crime Writers of Canada Best Juvenile or YA Crime Book. Her other books include *The Metro Dogs of Moscow*, which was a co-winner of the Chocolate Lily Award, *The Circus Dogs of Prague*, a finalist for the Pacific Northwest Library Association Young Reader's Choice Award, and *Clara Voyant*, a finalist for the Red Cedar and Chocolate Lily awards. She lives in Vancouver, BC. Visit her at rachelledelaney.com.

Author photograph by Claudette Carracedo